It's Never Too Late to Be a Bridesmaid

By Heather Estay

IT'S NEVER TOO LATE TO BE A BRIDESMAID
IT'S NEVER TOO LATE TO GET A LIFE

It's Never Too Late to Be a Bridesmaid

Heather Estay

AVON
TRADE

An Imprint of HarperCollinsPublishers

FIRST EDITION

Interior text designed by Elizabeth M. Glover

Library of Congress Cataloging-in-Publication Data

Estay, Heather.
  It's never too late to be a bridesmaid / by Heather Estay.—1st ed.
    p. cm.
ISBN-13: 978-0-06-076272-8 (acid-free paper)
ISBN-10: 0-06-076272-1 (acid-free paper)
1. Mothers and daughters—Fiction. 2. Divorced mothers—Fiction. 3. Weddings—Fiction.   I. Title.

PS3605.S73I67 2006
813'.6—dc22

2005016562

06 07 08 09 10 JTC/RRD 10 9 8 7 6 5 4 3 2 1

For my two sisters,
Laurie and Hawley:
I'll always value our differences
and cherish our love for one another.
Between the three of us,
we've got one husband,
two sons, and six dogs.
(I figure the ratios are just about right.)
Love,
Het

Acknowledgments

Once again, many thanks to: my personal Avon ladies, Carrie Feron and Selina McLemore, for cheerfully keeping me on track through this mysterious publication process (You need *what* by *when?*); Wendy Sherman, who never seems to lose my phone number nor her faith in me; and all of my golf buddies, choir buddies, Soroptimist buddies, and miscellaneous buddy buddies. You make my life sparkle with your love and laughter!

Prologue

So there I was being interviewed by Paris Hilton on *Paris Hilton Live!*

This, of course, was not merely a dream but a ghastly, nasty nightmare. Because if Paris Hilton is ever given her own talk show, that would certainly signal the end of civilization as we know it.

"So, um, Angie Hawkins, is it? So, is your life always this crazy?" Ms. Hilton raises a perfectly plucked eyebrow, runs a bejeweled hand through hair. Audience laughs appreciatively.

"No! Not at all! Before I left town, everything was fine. My daughter Jenna was self-confident and single. My son Tyler was rational and grounded. I had a few eligible men in my life. Well, actually, just one guy really, but I was keeping my options open." Hilton tosses her hair and directs significant look to camera. Audience murmurs. *"As for my best friends, Gwen was smart, Marie was nice, and Jessica . . . okay, so Jessica was never quite normal, but at least she was her own Jessica-self before I left."*

"Uh-huh. So, you're saying that it was mere coincidence that

everyone totally flipped out *when you, Angie Hawkins, callously left town and* abandoned *them!" Hilton turns to audience with appalled look. Audience gasps.*

"I didn't abandon them! I was out of town for a few days, but I was still there for them if they needed me!"

"Ha! But, you were not there there, were you? You were somewhere else there." *Hilton leans forward aggressively and moves in for the kill.*

"Uh, well, yes. I guess you could say that but . . ."

"And when you finally came home, you realized that everyone had gone stark raving mad!"

"Uh, perhaps 'raving,' but I don't know about 'stark' . . ."

"Admit it, Angie Hawkins: you were the only sane person left."

"Well, 'sane' is a relative term . . ."

"And so you took it upon yourself to poke your nose into everyone's business, thinking you could fix it all."

"Well, that was the plan but . . ."

"But you totally screwed things up, didn't you?"

"Well, I wouldn't say totally . . ."

"Ha! But what about the wedding?"

"What about it?"

"Single-handedly, Angie Hawkins, you nearly destroyed the wedding plans, didn't you?"

"Uh . . ."

"And almost got yourself squished to death in the process, right?"

"Well . . ."

"Then you landed in jail, right?"

"Yes, but that was another . . ."

"Got attacked by a vat of boiled icing?"

"Well, it didn't really . . ."

"Then you ended up on your butt singing in that hayloft!"

"Yes, but it's not like it sounds . . ."

"And all this from a woman who wears . . ." Hilton pauses dramatically and points to my shoes, *"Naturalizers!" Audience gasps in shock.*

Look, you can either hear Paris Hilton's version (a woman who can't manage to find the OFF button on a video camera) or mine (a woman who has flossed three times per day since Sonny first sang with Cher). If you want to hear mine, we need to start at the beginning. Can't you just hear Rod Serling introducing this?

"A town. An ordinary town, like Sacramento. Where friends are friends, men are available, children behave, and bridal showers are not lethal. But imagine: Angie Hawkins, middle-aged, post soccer mom, leaves this ordinary town for one brief, innocent business trip. And when she returns, she enters . . . *The Twilight Zone.*"

(If this is ever made into a movie, do *not* let Paris Hilton play my part.)

Chapter 1

It all started Friday evening when I returned to Sacramento with that delicious "there's no place like home" feeling. As I climbed into my own cozy bed, clicking my heels together three times in gratitude, I happily realized I had only one thing on my To-Do list for the following day:

Break in Tennies

I know what you're thinking: *Good grief! Nobody calls them tennies anymore!* They are cross-trainers or running shoes or air-lifts-with-gel-heels-and-neon-strikes (high-tech, vigorous labels allowing retailers to charge 300 percent more than they could for mere tennies). I know it's un-cool to call them tennies, but I just can't remember how this particular pair should be classified within the Periodic Table of Athletic Shoes. The pair I wanted to break in was On Sale and Comfy (my only criteria for any new shoes), and I bought them because my personal trainer Frank thinks that a new pair of shoes might keep me from falling off those unwieldy weight machines at the gym. Unlikely. Poor Frank is not yet willing to admit that some of us are intrinsically klutzy. Not even Super Glue will keep us attached to things that move.

I know you are also thinking: *This woman must have no life at all if the high point of her Saturday is to walk around in two pairs of socks to break in new shoes.*

Yep, you'd be right. I no longer have minivans full of wriggling midget soccer teams to cart all over Sacramento. I no longer have a potbellied husband who needs me to locate his socks or make his dinner ("Grilled cheese. Extra fries. And I'll take it in front of the TV, hon."). I am empty nested in all sorts of ways, and my time is totally (almost) my own to do with as I wish. I can devote an entire Saturday to breaking in new shoes or waxing my bikini area (typically not required since I've not worn a bikini since 1978) or doing the *New York Times* crossword puzzle in ink (about as likely as that bikini waxing thing). I have time, precious time, all to myself, which I hadn't had during the prior twenty-six years of being married and raising children. Eat your heart out.

Oh, not that I would have rewritten the past. I adore my kids and enjoyed every minute (well, most minutes) of raising them. And the husband, Bob, was okay for the most part, though I ended up breathing a sigh of relief when he ran off with the Neighborhood Watch captain, the lovely and slightly larger than a Winnebago Clarisse. But that was then, and this is now, and I don't want those days back.

So to return to my perfectly planned Saturday: It would start with a leisurely wake-up at about 10:00 A.M. Spud and Alli, my ever-loyal, never-grown-up beagles would miraculously sleep through their designated breakfast hour (this was *my* fantasy, so I can be as unrealistic as I like) and stay snuggled next to me like two fur-covered hot water bottles. At 10:00 A.M., I would stretch a leisurely stretch and head to the kitchen to make myself a latte, then . . . Great plan, huh? Of course it never happened.

What happened was that the shrill peal of my telephone shattered my cozy slumber at 3:32 A.M. Saturday morning, frightening my fur-covered hot water bottles into a barking frenzy. I grabbed for the receiver in a panic. Calls at 3:32 A.M. are not good news. Ed McMahon from the Publishers Clearinghouse Sweepstakes does not call at 3:32 A.M. That attractive guy you met last week doesn't phone to ask you out for coffee at 3:32 A.M. My son Tyler does not call to invite me to dinner and Jenna doesn't call to chat at 3:32 A.M.—3:32 A.M. is the time of emergencies.

"Annn-geee!"

"What? Who is this?"

"Annn-geee! Uh count fine num!"

"What? I can't understand you. Take a deep breath and speak slowly."

The person on the other end was either sobbing uncontrollably or speaking in a strange foreign tongue with a mouthful of peanut butter. I couldn't yet tell if the voice was male or female, someone I knew or an extremely annoying wrong number. Could it be the latest marketing scheme to sell long-distance phone service? The gears in my brain made ugly grinding noises as they struggled to engage. But as the mother of two kids now in their twenties, phone calls in the middle of the night from a sobbing, as-yet-unidentified person are not completely out of my experience.

"Okay. Take it easy. Who is this? Just say your name slowly."

"Gah-when!"

"Gwen? Oh my gosh! Are you okay? Has there been an accident? Where are you?" Gwen is one of my oldest (as in: she's known me since I figured out how to put in a diaphragm) and dearest (as in: I will always fight the urge to strangle her) friends. She's a brilliant attorney, and so calm and collected that you wonder if she had some kind of operation to remove the fluster response. I had *never* heard Gwen sobbing like this. In fact, I think I've only seen her crying once. It was the day that John Lennon died, which obviously heralded the end of all significant music, so her tears then were totally understandable. But hysterical sobbing? It had to be a Code Blue emergency. I started dressing with the phone balanced between my ear and my right shoulder.

"Gwen, are you bleeding?"

"Unh-unh."

"Good. Okay, but where does it hurt? Have you called 911?"

"Unh. Unh. Angie, I can't find them!" And she started wailing again.

"Can't find what? Gwen, what is it that you can't find?" Oh my gosh! Is she on some kind of lifesaving drug? I racked my brain trying to remember if Gwen is asthmatic, diabetic, prone to heart problems, or susceptible to the debilitating Vulcan Bendii Syndrome. (Vulcan Bendii Syndrome? Isn't it scary that we can't remember our own fax numbers, yet our minds tenaciously retain fictitious diseases from *Star Trek?* Or character names from ancient TV shows? Let's see, there was Wally, the Beaver, June, and that whiney kid . . .)

"My car keys! I can't find my car keys!" Her sobbing rose to the high pitch favored by mourners at Elvis memorials. (Marshal Dillon, Miss Kitty, Festus . . .) Did she say "car keys"? I was halfway into my jeans, but I paused.

"Your car keys? Gwen, do you need to go somewhere? At 3:32, uh, 3:34 in the morning?"

"No! But on Mon . . . mon . . . daaay!"

Let's see. It was Friday night (okay, so I know they call 3:34 A.M. Saturday morning, but honestly doesn't it really belong to Friday night? I mean if you are up at 3:34, uh, 3:35 A.M., you are probably still drinking martinis and not ordering eggs over easy, right?). Gwen could not find her car keys to get somewhere on Monday, two whole days away. So where's the crisis? I obviously had stumbled into the middle of a Fellini movie, missing some critical plot information.

"Okay, Gwen. You lost your car keys. It's now, uh, 3:36 on Saturday morning. Don't you think you'll have time to locate them before Monday? Or couldn't you call a cab to pick you up?"

"Angie, you are so lame!" Actually, she said "la la la aim!" and started hiccupping in between sobs. But the fact that she could insult me was a good sign. One of the basic dynamics of our relationship is Gwen's impatience with my inability to follow her lightning-fast intellect. I'm not stupid (though I'll admit I'm not my sharpest at 3:38 A.M.), but at any time of day, few people can match Gwen's brilliant mind.

"Angie, the problem is that my brain has completely stopped functioning! I've never lost my car keys before! I've never lost anything before!" She gulped for air which only served to increase her already earsplitting volume. "I can't figure out what to wear Monday or where I'm supposed to be tomorrow or how the 1976 ruling for Chandler *v.* Roudebush will affect my client's case. I can't remember if I've picked up my dry cleaning, I can't remember the combination on my safe-deposit box, and I can't find my car keys!"

"Gwen, lots of people forget little things like that. I can't remember if I picked up my dry cleaning either." In fact, which dry cleaner did I use last time? Was it the one around the corner with the nice Korean lady or the one near my office with the bad parking lot?

"Angie, that kind of fuzzy, blurry thinking is normal for you. It is not for me. How could I even function if I walked around as half-baked as you do?"

Gwen's healthy signs of insulting me were getting too healthy for my taste. Especially at 3:41 A.M. Under normal circumstances, I would have told her so. But Gwen sobbing in the middle of the night is definitely not normal. I sat back on the bed, jeans at my ankles.

"Gwen, did this all just happen tonight?"

"Yes. No. There have been several times lately when I can't seem to think through the simplest issue from A to Z. I get to J or M and lose the thread. Sometimes I make it to R. But just this morning, I found myself lost at around F . . ." Her voice trailed off, misplacing itself somewhere around K, I believe. This did not sound good. "Maybe I should marry Wayne after all. So he can take care of me."

"Marry Wayne?" I asked puzzled. Wayne was Gwen's long-term, long-distance boyfriend. Though he is a charming man, I believe the long distance has contributed significantly to the long term. "Did he ask you to marry him?"

"Yes. About seven years ago, I think."

I decided not to bring up the possibility that his proposal might have passed its statute of limitations. "Okay, Gwen. I'm on my way over. We'll find your car keys, and we'll look at your Palm Pilot together and figure out where you need to be on Monday and how to get you there." And I'll sing you the alphabet song to calm you down.

"Angie, don't be ridiculous! You can't come over now. It's the middle of the night for God's sake! I'm exhausted, and I'm going back to bed to get some sleep. Call me later at a more reasonable hour." And with that, Gwen hung up.

Oh. I see. So Gwen, who had the opportunity to sob her heart out to one of her very best friends, was now cried out and sleepy and heading off to dreamland. Of course that left one of her very best friends, me, with jangled nerves and absolutely no possibility of getting back to sleep.

I climbed back into bed, or rather into that little space of my bed that remained unoccupied. Spud had stretched his twenty-pound frame perpendicularly across three-quarters of our queen-sized mattress. Alli had snuggled herself into the warm spot I had vacated, forty pounds of sleeping canine that surely weighed ten times that much when I tried to scoot her over a few inches. I scrunched my body creatively around the beagles and nabbed a corner of pillow. Now to sleep.

Okay. Sleep. Now to sleep. Spud and Alli snored in harmony as I stared at the ceiling. Don't turn on the light. Sleep will come. It has to come. Just be patient.

I am an Olympic sleeper; it's one of my few real talents. My ability to sleep through anything is legendary. This reputation as a Master Sleeper was solidified when I dozed off in front of the TV just as the verdict in the OJ Simpson trial was being announced. I snoozed through most of my honeymoon (for reasons we don't need to go into), and I even slept soundly during my kids' teenage years (despite some very bizarre dreams involving padded cells and chastity belts). Even in the rough months after my divorce, I slept pretty well, though more often than not I cried myself to sleep. I simply never have insomnia.

And the problem with simply never having insomnia is that I have absolutely no idea what to do about it. Should I drink warm milk? Whose disgusting idea was that? Count sheep? Why sheep? I've never been a farm girl, but I understand that sheep are not only incredibly stupid (so probably have trouble organizing themselves to be counted) but they're also pretty mangy. Maybe sheepherders can't bathe them because they would shrink. Can sheep be dry-cleaned?

This line of thought was getting me nowhere, so I did

what every inexperienced insomniac does: I tossed and turned until my jammies wrapped around me like ribbons on a maypole, periodically sneaked a peek at the clock to ensure that—yes, indeedy!—time was moving forward, and searched my mental data bank for something to worry about. I thought of the kids first, of course. Aren't worry and children practically synonymous? Over the years, I had filled many hours of fruitless worry time using the kids as subjects, so it was familiar territory.

But both kids were doing well right now. Jenna was thrilled with her work, though I wasn't thrilled that she spent her days wrestling with thousand-pound creatures in slimy muddy arenas. She's not an oversized lady mud wrestler; my lovely 110-pound princess is in training to be a large animal veterinarian. Jenna loves it, and her social life was picking up as well. She was happily and steadily dating her boss, a veterinarian who shares her fascination with the health and care of cow udders and sheep colons.

Tyler, my son, had just started his career as an attorney, his dream since elementary school. Driving himself all through school, college, and law school to attain it, he had put social life on the back burner. But recently, Tyler had inaugurated his dating career with a blond lingerie model, a young woman named Cyndee who perfectly fits every stereotype you might have about such a person. Cyndee would not have been my first choice for Tyler, but what young man ever dates his mom's favorite candidate? So I bit my tongue—and would undoubtedly bite it clean off if he ever decided to promote Cyndee to daughter-in-law.

So the kids were okay. But Gwen? Obviously, there was

something to worry about there. But what? Had she been drunk? No, Gwen is neither a sloppy, nor a frequent, drunk. She's more of a once-every-decade, Socrates-spouting drunk. So what could be upsetting her? As of two weeks ago, when she stepped out of her Jag to meet me for lunch, she was the epitome of "having it all": a nationally respected law practice, an enviable relationship (a long-distance one which, to some, made it more enviable), and a wardrobe that would make Coco Chanel jealous. (Granted, Coco has been dead for over thirty years. But a wardrobe like Gwen's could draw any fashion-conscious woman from her grave.) Why would Gwen suddenly want to change all that and get married?

Something must have set her off, but what? Losing your car keys is certainly not cause for hysteria. I lose my own car keys every now and then. In fact, where did I stash those keys last night? And the extra set of keys? That flash-light I keep for emergencies, where was that? (Barney, Aunt Bee, Opie . . .) Where did I put that instruction man-ual for my new barbecue? The clock told me that it was 4:37.

Dawn was just dawning as I drifted off to sleep, itemiz-ing everything I had put in a very safe place that I was pretty sure I could no longer locate. The mind is a won-drous thing. (Jed, Granny, Elly May, Jethro, that sour sec-retary . . . what was her name?)

Chapter 2

Marie burst through my front door exactly twenty-four minutes later disrupting my brief taste of a delicious early-morning snooze. I definitely need to find friends who keep more regular hours. Not only was it unusual that Marie burst through my front door unannounced (she is a very considerate neighbor/landlord and always knocks), but I don't think I've ever seen Marie burst through anything. She's just not the bursting type. She's more the move slowly and with grace type.

"Angie, I hate him!" she bellowed. She is also not the bellowing type.

"Which him?" I lifted my head from the pillow and opened one eye reluctantly. Spud slowly extricated himself from under the covers, his tail wagging sleepily. He gave me a look that indicated that my friends could use a little more obedience training.

"Jack, of course! He's a brute and an idiot, and I can't stand the sight of him!"

Huh? I hadn't seen Marie for a little over a week, but at that time she still worshipped the ground Jack walked on. In their ten years of marriage, I can't remember her ever being critical of him. Quite the contrary; typically Marie gushes about Jack like Annette Funicello gushed about Frankie Avalon: Dreamboat, Stud Muffin, Heartthrob—labels I hadn't heard since junior high. Personally, I doubt that Jack will ever be recruited to join the Chippendales, even the Senior Circuit Chippendales, but he truly is one of the all-time great guys. A retired judge, he is kind and charming, humorous and interesting. And Jack is totally enamored with Marie, as she is with him—or at least as she was with him until this morning.

"Marie, that doesn't sound like Jack. Are you sure . . . ?"

"Of course I am! Angie, never let a man come close to your heart because he'll break it in two!" And with that she started banging around my kitchen, slamming doors, clanging pots.

Because I live in a tiny studio guest cottage—Marie and Jack's tiny studio guest cottage—banging around in my kitchen is like the *1812 Overture* played at full volume within the confines of an army tank. (In truth, I've never been in an army tank, so this is pure speculation.)

"Marie, what are you doing?"

"Making coffee." I'd never heard coffee made so ballistically before, and though I did crave some caffeine, I wasn't sure my kitchen would survive her efforts.

"What happened, Marie? What could Jack possibly have done to get you so upset?" And make you so raucous this early in the morning?

"He . . . he left the toilet seat up!" She slammed a pot down so ferociously that even Alli, the champion of all sleepers, woke up with a startled yelp.

Okay, so I know that the toilet seat thing can be unsettling. One of the bonuses of being recently divorced is knowing that I am no longer at risk of landing on the cold porcelain of an unseated toilet during an emergency bathroom run in the middle of the night. But her reaction seemed a little extreme. Maybe she fell in?

"Marie, this hardly seems cause for . . ."

"Angie, don't you see? This was intentional! Jack is having an affair!"

The leap from misplaced toilet seat to an illicit affair was a pretty long one. "Um, Marie, what leads you to believe . . . ?"

"Don't be dense, Angie! Jack has never been this inconsiderate before! It's obvious that he no longer cares about me."

At this, I forced myself to sit up to scrutinize the pot-banger in the kitchen carefully (which unfortunately required me to open my eyes—both of them—all the way) to verify that she really was Marie. Because besides not being a burster, a bellower, or a pot-banger, I have never known Marie to leap to conclusions. The Marie I have known for many years considers life deeply and with great insight. She thinks carefully before speaking. She gives everyone the benefit of the doubt, and, whether you like it or not, she can find rational explanations for even the most heinous of actions.

This person crashing around my kitchen was like the real

Marie's Dark Evil Twin: angry, unreasonable, and very, very noisy. I just hoped that this Dark Evil Twin could make as good a cup of coffee as the real Marie can. I could tell I was going to need it.

Except for the ferocious scowl on her face, the woman in my kitchen looked like Marie: generously curvy body, long, wavy, dark hair, deep smoky eyes. She seemed familiar with my kitchen, and Spud and Alli lay trustingly at her feet in give-me-tummy-rub position. This last fact proved nothing; beagles will indiscriminately solicit tummy rubs from just about anyone, even Dark Evil Twins. Charmers they are; guard dogs they are not.

"Marie," I said as I dragged myself out of bed and into my bathrobe, "let's take it from the beginning. Was there some other incident besides the toilet seat thing?"

"Of course! Three days ago, he didn't even touch me when we went to bed. Said he had a bad cold or something, can you believe it? In all our years together, we've never gone to bed without . . ."

"Well, maybe he really did have a bad cold," I interrupted quickly. Marie has always hinted that her sex life with Jack is pretty, uh, robust. But it was way too early in the day to hear the X-rated details. "And one night doesn't prove anything." I also wanted to add that any guy who is sixty-seven deserves a night off once in a while. But I wasn't sure how good Marie's aim might be if she decided to throw one of those pots she was still banging.

"Well, what about this one? Yesterday, he brought up the idea of renewing our vows for our anniversary." Marie, hands on hips, glared at me significantly.

"Uh, right. And that means . . . ?" I felt like Inspector Clouseau: *That is why I have always failed where others have succeeded.*

"Obviously, Jack is feeling guilty about something." Obviously? Where was the obviously part? "And it's not just that. There have been a thousand other subtle signs, Angie. A woman knows these things."

Frankly, I had recently proven to the world that I am a woman who clearly does *not* know these things, so it was hard for me to comment. My ex, Bob, had conducted an affair for months only two blocks from home, and I never figured it out. I just thought it odd that he was so enthusiastic about the Neighborhood Watch committee meetings, carefully lacquering and combing his three strands of hair, tucking in his shirt over his bulging belly, and even wearing cologne in preparation. Frankly, I should have guessed something was up when he was willing to miss *Buffy the Vampire Slayer* every week to attend. But I didn't. The word "clueless" was definitely coined for me.

"I know what the problem is, Angie. Jack just doesn't find me attractive anymore."

"That's ridiculous, Marie! Jack adores you, and you're a beautiful woman!"

"Oh, I know I'm good-enough-looking, Angie, for my age. Hear that? For my age." Marie's eyes teared up, but she seemed more angry and frustrated than sad. She slammed down her coffee cup, rattling my tiny kitchen table. "Face it, Angie. I just don't have 'it' anymore."

"What 'it'?"

"Sex appeal. I'm just too damn old to be sexy anymore."

"Marie, you're crazy! You are undoubtedly one of the sexiest women I know!" And I wasn't just saying it to save my crockery. Marie has an amazing natural sensuality that would certainly be banned by the Conservative Right as an illicit drug if it could be bottled and sold. Imagine Catherine Zeta-Jones, twenty years older and a few pounds more curvy—that's Marie. She's in her early fifties, but I swear I've seen seventeen-year-old boys stampede to the checkout stand for the honor of bagging her groceries. Like some captivating Greek goddess, Marie has always had her pick of any man around. And Jack, dear Jack, had always known that he was the luckiest man in the world to be the one she had chosen.

"Maybe I had it once, Angie. But that kind of thing has an age limit, and I've passed it."

"What are you talking about? There are plenty of women older than you who are still hot. Look at Ann-Margret. Look at Catherine Deneuve, Jacqueline Bisset. Look at Cher."

"Angie, Cher doesn't count. She's been nipped, tucked, and surgically enhanced so often that she probably has no original body parts left. She's like a rebuilt '57 Chevy."

"Okay, well, what about Barbie? Barbie just celebrated her fifty-fifth birthday. Has Barbie lost her appeal? I don't think so." There was a long pause. I smugly sipped my coffee, knowing I had finally scored a point.

"Angie, Barbie is a doll."

"Oh, right. I knew that." I remained scoreless.

"Face it, Angie. Older women just aren't considered sexy. Take Diane Keaton. She was buck naked in that scene with Jack Nicholson, and they didn't even give the movie an X rating! Obviously, no one thinks a totally nude fifty-eight-year-old woman is sexy enough to be a threat."

"But Diane Keaton's got a great body, Marie, and Keanu Reaves was hot for her, right?"

"Get real, Angie! It was in the script. He was just acting."

"Well, he must have felt some attraction to be so convincing in the movie."

"No, he didn't. He's a professional actor. Like that kid in *Harold and Maude*. Do you really believe that kid thought Ruth Gordon was sexy?"

"Well, uh . . ." I couldn't believe that Marie and I were actually arguing about characters in movies and actors we'd never met and never would meet. "Marie, that's not the point. The point is that you still have more than your share of 'it.' "

"You wouldn't understand, Angie. You're still in your prime." She looked at me accusingly.

"But I'm only three years younger than you are! How can I possibly be in my prime when you're over the . . ."

"It happens quickly, Angie. And when it does, you're instantly an old hag that nobody wants. Thanks for the coffee." With that, Marie slammed her cup down and stomped out the door.

I sat stunned for a few moments. Had what just happened really happened? Had I ever seen Marie so . . . so . . . enraged? If so, I can't remember it. In fact she's the only woman I've ever known who didn't try to vivisect her husband during labor. (That had been the husband before Jack; he had definitely deserved vivisection and many other forms of bodily injury for more than one reason.) Marie's customary patience and kindness would have qualified her for sainthood (except she's Presbyterian, and I don't think they offer that rank).

This kindness had been extended to me after my divorce settlement. (Why the heck do they call it a divorce "settlement" anyway? Mine had left me totally *un*settled, both financially and emotionally.) Marie had offered me a home in her little guesthouse, which had been a godsend. The plan was for me to stay here for a few months, just long enough to get my feet back under me. But the months had passed quickly, and I found myself still in residence after nearly a year. It had been so comfortable and peaceful here—until that morning.

Finally, I got up, fed the pups, and poured myself another cup of the Dark Evil Twin's very good coffee. Obviously, my relaxing, happily self-centered weekend with nothing to do was going to be a bit more complicated than originally anticipated. So I did what every expert multitasker, Soccer Mom to Corporate Powerhouse, does: I revised my To-Do list.

> *Break in Tennies*
> *Go Visit Gwen*
> *Do Something Nice for Marie*
> *Take a LONG Nap*

There. Now even though my uncooperative brain had stripped its gears and was trying to roll back into bed, I felt more organized. That's when I noticed that my message light was blinking furiously, apparently missed in my eagerness to climb into my cozy bed the previous night. (Have you ever seen an answering machine with a calm, unperturbed blink? Me neither. In blink language, it must be equivalent to shouting, "Hey! Where have you been? While you've been out gallivanting around, this phone has been ringing off the hook! The least you can do is pick up your messages! Now! I said now!") My first message was from Jenna:

"Mom, are you free for dinner Saturday night? I have some good news. I'll be at your place around six . . ."

The second was from Jess, the third of my three best friends:

"Angie, you absolutely have to join me for lunch Saturday! I have something I'm dying to share with you! I absolutely won't take no for an answer! Meet me at . . ."

Oh. Okay, no problem. Simply revise my To-Do list:

Break in Tennies
~~Go visit~~=CALL Gwen
~~Do Something Nice For~~=CALL Marie
Take a ~~LONG~~ SHORT nap
Look in <u>Bon Apetit</u> for new recipes for Jenna dinner
Buy groceries
Meet Jess for Lunch

I climbed back into bed with my coffee, knowing that the odds of my getting back to sleep had gone from "Somewhat Unlikely" to "Don't Kid Yourself." But I closed my eyes just in case I could sneak in a short snooze. Doing so, of course, caused the phone to ring.

"Hey, Sunshine." I smiled to hear Tim's voice, as warm and welcome as a hug.

No one having real experience with me in the morning has ever called me "Sunshine." Tim, relatively new in my life, had not yet personally witnessed my waking up in the morning. Like the Monster from the Blue Lagoon emerging from the swamp, it's a slow process and not pretty. There's the groaning part, then the stumbling, the face scrunching, the yawning—well, you get the picture. Under normal circumstances and with a full eight hours of sleep, it takes me several minutes and at least two cups of very strong coffee to surface from the swamp muck of a deep sleep. Without my full quota of sleep? Forget it. My body may rise, but my mind may not totally emerge for the whole day. Still, Tim's voice gave me a warm glow, awakening at least a couple of areas of my body.

"Hey yourself, Tim. Back in town?"

"Yeah. You okay, Angie? You sound pretty wiped out."

"Hmmmm. Wild night last night." Tim was silent as he tried to interpret "wild night." I couldn't elaborate further; even a swamp monster knows how to be discreet. I wasn't about to discuss Gwen's and Marie's bizarre behavior to someone they hardly knew.

"Oh. Well, wild nights happen, huh?" he offered, still fishing. I wanted to explain that wild nights of any sort do *not* typically happen to me. I wanted to explain that this wild night was not particularly fun. I wanted to explain that if he wanted to join me in a wild night sometime, we could . . . oh my gosh! Did I say that out loud?

"So, Angie, are you free for dinner? I thought we could head down to the river."

"That would have been great, Tim, but I'm seeing Jenna for dinner tonight."

"Tomorrow night then?"

"Sorry, I've got plans with Tyler."

"Oh." Another silence.

I really like Tim. He's got a killer smile that, even on half power, makes me giddy. When he turns it on full power, I fully understand what inspires women to throw their intimate clothing on stage during Julio Iglesias concerts. (However, what I don't understand is where that underwear comes from. Do they bring an extra pair of panties to the concert? Or is it the panties they're wearing? And if they're wearing them, how the heck do they get them off in the crowd? And how exactly do you throw them to be sure that they land onstage and not on the head of the bald guy two rows down? And what about size? I mean, if the real bra size is too small or the real panty size too large to be erotic, do you go out and buy them in a different size for throwing purposes?) As I said, I really like Tim.

But on the downside, Tim travels a lot and these last-minute invitations that I couldn't accept were all too common. Does he think I sit around, waiting for him to call? That I have no other life? Am I supposed to cancel everything just because he deigns to ask me out? Am I so unimportant to him that he calls only when he has nothing better to do? If he really cared, he would . . .

"So, Angie, is there any chance we could get together within the next few days? I'd really like to spend some time with you, and I've got something I want to talk to you about. I have to leave town again next Thursday. I'd really like to see you before I go."

Aw, how sweet! And very Tim-like. Just when I get irritated at him, he shows how much potential he might have, given the proper care and training of course.

"Uh, maybe brunch tomorrow? Say around eleven?"

"We could do that. I know a place in the foothills where they have . . ." Tim and I talked for a few more minutes, him being charming and witty, me straining to keep my brain from sinking into sweet unconsciousness of the Blue Lagoon.

Rerevised To-Do List:
~~Break in Tennies~~
~~Go visit~~=CALL Gwen after dinner
~~Do Something Nice For~~ CALL Marie
Take a ~~LONG~~ SHORT nap
Look in <u>Bon Apetit</u> *for ~~new recipes for dinner~~*
   old Coq Au Vin recipe
Buy groceries
Meet Jess for Lunch
Find new outfit for brunch with Tim

I grudgingly pulled myself out of bed with a wistful look at my still-pristine tennies and my hardly rumpled sheets. Spud and Alli, having no To Do list screaming for their attention, climbed back into bed to watch me while I unpacked, showered, and dressed. With a few minutes to spare (those useless little minutes when it's too early to leave but not enough time to do something productive), I puttered around at my tiny home, all 450 square feet of it, and mused about my fledgling love life.

There wasn't much to muse about. After twenty-six years of marriage, "getting out there" again wasn't even in the same zip code as my comfort zone. But my three best friends had coaxed, cajoled, and coerced me into it. They had sent me on a few blind dates (The horrifying thing about blind dates, beyond the fact that these dates are invariably horrifying in themselves, is that it's like a Rorschach ink blot test: The blind date people choose for you reveals *exactly* what they think of you) and insisted that I keep a list of "viable romantic options," a list that thus far only had three names on it. Tim, by far, was the most promising of the bunch. He's a great kisser, has a smile that could inspire lobbing undies in public, and, with just a few tweaks here and there, might even be marriage material.

But I was determined to take it slow, keep my options open, and wait for a truly extraordinary relationship, like the ones in Jane Austen novels and Cole Porter songs. Improbable? Probably. Impossible? No. Just look at Jack and Marie.

I know it's voyeuristic, but I love watching Jack and Marie together, dancing at their favorite jazz hangout, holding hands as they walk down the street, smiling secret little smiles at each other in a crowd. They didn't need a ceremony to renew their vows; they did it in each moment together. Too mushy, you think? Jack and Marie's mush is sweet and sincere with just enough intensity to remain interesting, like the air sizzling just after a thunderstorm.

Honestly, wouldn't most of us renounce our most cherished vice (not *that* one, but the one manufactured by Ben & Jerry) to experience that depth of affection, passion, and romance? Jack and Marie's relationship had been an inspiration reminding me that, though I'd not found extraordinary love in my first marriage, it was definitely possible the second time around.

And that's another reason why Marie's tantrum was so unnerving; if Marie and Jack couldn't make it, who could?

Chapter 3

Honestly, though I love Jessica, she is not my most normal of friends. Jessica is "out there" even by California standards, which says a lot. If you want to hear about the Kennedy clan conspiracy to undermine the Republican party using bodybuilders, talk to Jessica. If you are wondering which phase of the moon is most beneficial for making good chili con carne, Jessica can tell you. If you are curious about the ultimate fate of all those socks that get eaten in the laundry, Jessica can enlighten you (I think it has something to do with black holes and the origin of the universe, but don't quote me on that). However, typically, if you are looking for a little calm and quiet, peace and normalcy, Jess is not the first person you should seek out.

But when I spotted Jess across the crowded restaurant, she looked to be the perfect picture of peaceful normalcy. In fact, she was holding hands affectionately with a nice-looking young man, and I remembered that one of her sons, the one who works as a consultant for one of the Big Six (Big Five? Big Three?) accounting firms in New York, was back in town for a few months. He and Jessica looked so sweet and loving together!

As I worked my way over to the table, I dredged up memories of Jessica's sons. Jess and I had met in Lamaze class more than twenty years ago, and our children had played together as toddlers. But because her sons had moved to New York to be with their father, Jess's ex, I hadn't seen any of them in years. This one looked to be in his midtwenties, about Tyler's age. I racked my brain for his name but drew a complete blank. So I did what every intelligent, mature, self-assured woman would do in this situation. I faked it.

"Oh, my goodness! Look at you! What a surprise! I'm so glad to see you!" I enthused and gushed my way through the awkward moment, giving Jess's boy a big hug and a kiss on the cheek. I thought I'd pulled it off pretty well, though he looked vaguely surprised and bewildered as I sat down.

"Angie," Jess beamed, "this is Chad."

"How do you do, Angie?" Chad said politely, reaching across the table to shake my hand.

Chad? The name Chad didn't ring a bell, but I was running on far too little sleep for any internal bell ringing. Maybe it was a new nickname he'd adopted, or a political statement from the 2000 election. But how did he pick up that British accent in New York?

"I'm delighted to see you, Chad. How is your father?"

"You know my father?"

"Sure. It's been many years but . . ."

"Angie, that's amazing!" Jess broke in excitedly.

"It is?"

"Absolutely! Isn't it incredible how the Cosmos creates all of these serendipitous connections? I mean, I just met Chad a month ago, and we just started seeing each other last week, and you actually know his father!" Jessica beamed with the wonderful Cosmic Serendipity of it all, Chad looked even more confused, and I flipped over an entire basket of bread sticks as I ducked under the table to hide my reaction.

They were "seeing each other"? Jessica was dating this . . . this . . . kid? Jess is a grandmother, for heaven's sake! Of course, she doesn't look it. Petite and delicate, with a naturally radiant complexion, most people assume she's in her late thirties. But underneath all of those non-existent wrinkles, she's still fiftysomething. This Chad guy probably hadn't even hit the Big Three-O.

I'm not absolutely sure that I have a really good poker face. I know that I have one when I'm actually playing poker. However, this is only because I can never remember what cards win over what other cards, so my face remains appropriately blank. But how about when I'm shocked, and I'm not supposed to show it? How can you really test that out? Do you stand in front of a mirror and study your face as you say something outrageously blasphemous to yourself? Like a self-tickle treatment, I can't believe that would really work.

In any event, I had no mirror with me under that table and figured I couldn't remain hidden there forever. In an attempt to neutralize my face, I conjured up the image of a poker hand (two jacks, a queen, two tens—is that good?). I focused all my brainpower on determining if this was or was not a winning hand as I surfaced from under the table, knocking over my water glass as I did.

"So sorry. Dropped my napkin. So, isn't this nice! Here we are!" I babbled blithely, visualizing clubs and spades as I sopped up my latest mess. Chad rose abruptly, undoubtedly wary of what Jessica's demented friend might do next.

"Well, my love, I'm afraid I must run." He kissed the inside of Jessica's wrist in a very *un*-son like gesture. She smiled seductively at him, then studied his backside brazenly as he left the restaurant. I cringed feeling embarrassed for her, like the embarrassment you feel for some guy who forgets to zip his zipper up. (Now what is the etiquette there exactly? Is it better to tell the poor sap? Does it depend on whether you know him or not? Or is it based on the status of his underwear? Can you just ignore it and remain silent, or is it one of those civic duty issues?)

"So, Angie," Jess turned to me beaming breathlessly, "what do you think of Chad?"

I hate this part. I don't think that you should always tell people exactly what you think, at least not until you've had a chance to think through exactly what you think so you can express it in a way that the person on the receiving end of your thoughts doesn't think you are thoughtless. Don't you think so?

"Oh, well, Jess, I've just now met him . . ."

"But you have a first impression, right?"

Sure. My first impression is that he probably was ditch-ing his high school algebra class to join us. That he is probably just learning to shave. That his mother is probably younger than we are. That he probably still gets carded at R-rated movies.

"Well, yes, Chad seems very, uh, attractive" (in a jail bait sort of way), "and, um, well-mannered" (acting with appropriate deference to his elders). Clearly, I was not covering well, so I tried to switch the subject. "But what happened to Whatsis Name?"

Whatsis Name had been Jessica's live-in fiancé for the past couple of years. I suppose the fact that none of us, not even Jessica, could ever remember his name had not boded well for the potential of their relationship.

"Oh, Whatsis Name and I broke up weeks ago. He just couldn't keep up with me sexually."

"He couldn't what?" I spit out, along with my latest sip of water.

"Keep up sexually, especially in the last few months. I have definitely sensed my Tantric levels rising. And it is very unhealthy to deny the expression of the lower chakras when they are glowing. So rather than further frustrating my Inner Feminine with Whatsis Name, I decided to access Yang element of other sentient beings with more compatible energy flows."

Translating from Jessica-speak to English, she had decided to go out and get laid more often.

Four hours ago, I had been listening to Marie bemoan the fact that she is over-the-hill and no longer sexy. Jessica, a few years older than Marie, was so hot to trot that she was out seeking new young bones to jump. What was wrong with this picture? When would Allen Funt pop out and tell me to "Smile! You're on *Candid Camera!*"?

"But isn't, um, Chad just a bit, uh, youthful for you?"

"Don't tell me that you are so provincial that you're shocked when a woman dates a slightly younger man?"

"I'm not shocked," I protested. Though truthfully, I was shocked, and I questioned Jessica's math skills if she thought Chad was just "slightly" younger.

"Oh, Angie, you are so out of it!" Jess laughed indulgently. "Older women dating younger men is a very common situation nowadays. Look at Demi Moore and Ashton Kutcher, Mary Tyler Moore and Robert Levine, Susan Sarandon and Tim Robbins, Joan Collins and Percy Gibson."

"Harold and Maude?" I added helpfully.

Jessica ignored me. She had obviously prepared herself for this discussion. "Angie, haven't you noticed that men our age are slowing down in the getting it up department?"

I would not be called in as an expert witness on that particular question. In the year since I had been single again, I'd had exactly one hot fling (which turned out to be as successful as the maiden voyage of the *Titanic)*. Since then, I had done some heavy smooching with Tim, a little slow dancing with another guy (close enough that our name tags got hooked around each other), and shared coffee with a third (our hands definitely touched when he handed me my latté). In other words, I had a lot of hope for future research into Jessica's issue, but very little empirical data to contribute at this point.

Fortunately, when Jess gets talking, she can carry on a

conversation with very little input from me. So she did. Her voice in its natural state assaults the eardrums like a frantic car alarm. But that day Jess was excited, and when Jess is excited, you could use her as the National Early Warning Siren. Everyone within three square blocks had the privilege of hearing her dissertation.

"Angie, I believe that as we women age and embrace our Essential Feminine, we begin to exude a deep Earth Mother sensuality that is particularly attractive to young, virile men. Maybe men our own age are threatened by this deep sexuality and so perhaps lose their ability to perform in the face of our Isis power emerging . . ."

Jessica is unusual to say the least. Her interests are eclectic, and she has investigated just about every New Age and Ancient Age discipline and/or science existing. She has studied yoga and enneagrams, hydroponic gardening and Feng Shui. She's taken classes on ancient Vedic tradition, quantum physics, and detoxification via fasting. She's read the *I Ching*, the *Tibetan Book of the Dead*, and Stephen Hawking's *Universe in a Nutshell*.

On the other hand, she also reads *Star*, which recently exposed Donald Rumsfeld as a robot and Britney Spears as an extraterrestrial (stories which I personally find highly believable), cover to cover every week. Jess is certainly not stupid, but sometimes I wonder if she assumes that all printed material, whether it comes from the *National Enquirer* or *National Geographic*, is equally valid. We had an argument about this years ago:

"Angie, are you so narrow-minded that you think everything has to be verified by Western scientific methodologies?"

"No, of course not. But Jess, I just think there's a difference between information you can get out of the *Encyclopedia Britannica* and off the back of a Wheaties box."

"Wheaties boxes are very reputable, Angie. Did you know that Ronald Reagan was an announcer for Wheaties in the thirties?"

"Uh . . ."

"And he became president of the United States, didn't he? And what about Tiger Woods?"

"What about him?"

"He was on a Wheaties box and he went to Stanford, your old alma mater. See what I mean? Wouldn't you trust another Stanford grad?"

Sometimes I wonder if it would be easier to follow Jessica's logic after ingesting copious amounts of psychedelics.

Her piercing voice brought me back to the discussion (or monologue) at hand. "Besides, what if I decide to marry again someday? What's the sense in marrying a guy who's past his prime? Whose warranty is about to expire?"

Yeah, but you might want a groom who is old enough to sip champagne at his own wedding. "Jess, do you want to get married again?"

"Maybe. And if I do, I don't want to get stuck with some shriveled-up old codger with a shriveled-up old . . ."

"Jess," I interrupted quickly, "not all men our age have, uh, or are shriveled-up old, uh, things. What about Wayne? Or Tim?"

"Ah-ha! Tim proves my point. He's younger than you, isn't he?"

"Sure, by four months. Jess, I hardly think . . ." I was distracted from what I hardly thought because Jess convulsed suddenly in a violent shudder. She rubbed her arms furiously, as if trying to ward off the heebie-jeebies. (What is—are?—the heebie-jeebies anyway? And is it singular or plural? Can you have an individual heebee jeebie or do they always travel in packs?) "Jess, what's wrong?"

"Oh, it's nothing. This happens every so often lately. I'm fine, then all of a sudden I feel itchy all over."

"Is it poison oak or something?"

"Oh, no. I'm sure it has to do with the enhanced sexual energy flowing up my chakras and through my body."

"Tantric twitches?" I tried to stifle my giggles but didn't succeed.

"Laugh if you like, Angie. But if you wake up in the middle of the night in heat and all itchy and twitchy, you'll know what you need to do."

"Find myself a Chad? A dimpled Chad perhaps? Or a well-hung Chad?"

Jess, not appreciating my humor, merely scowled. Her face, delicate and petite, was not really designed for good scowling; she looked as ferocious as a kitten in bad temper.

"Aw, look, Jess, I'm sorry. It's been a rough day so far. I'm very glad that you're happy, okay?"

"Okay." She brightened immediately. "So let me tell you about this absolutely fantastic adult toy store Chad showed me yesterday . . ."

For the next forty-five minutes, I (along with most of the north side of Sacramento) was treated to enthusiastic descriptions of apparatus that would make Sally Rand blush. So, if I held three sevens and the ace of spades and . . .

~~Break in tennies~~
~~Go visit~~=CALL Gwen after dinner
~~Do Something Nice For~~=CALL Marie tomorrow
~~Take a LONG~~ SHORT nap
~~Look in Bon Apetit for new recipes for dinner old~~
    ~~Coq Au Vin recipe~~
Make Quick & Easy Garlic Chicken from
    <u>Good Housekeeping</u>
Buy groceries
✓ Meet Jess for Lunch
~~Buy new~~ Iron outfit for brunch with Tim
Rent <u>Harold and Maude</u> for Jessica

After lunch, I raced through my grocery shopping and dashed home in hopes of sneaking in a quick nap (ignoring the fact that my To-Do list had given it up as hopeless). But Jack was waiting for me at the front door. Uh-oh. I hoped he wasn't going to ask me about my conversation with Marie that morning. What had been his big offense? The heinous crime of the unseated toilet? The nefarious and highly suspicious suggestion that they renew their vows?

"Angie, if you have a minute, would you mind helping me? The electrical connections on track number five aren't working, and I need someone to help test them."

"Sure, Jack. Happy to help." I was flattered that Jack trusted me to assist in this highly technical task. Jack's the kind of guy who really respects women. He not only pulls out our chairs and opens doors for us. He also treats us as if we are at least as competent and intelligent as he is. I often wish he taught classes on the subject; I have several potential students for him. "What do I need to do?"

"I'll fool with the connections and you tell me if the light on the caboose comes on." Yep, just about my speed technology-wise.

We went into the basement, where Jack and his train club keep their display. The miniature world they created in Jack's basement is remarkable and magical. Six or seven tracks running through mountains, valleys, fruited plains (I couldn't actually see the fruit, but I'm sure it was there). The detail was incredible: the action of the tiny trains and railroad crossings, the lights in the miniature houses, the clocks in the bell towers that kept time. If every kid had one of these in his/her basement, I'll bet early-juvenile crime would plummet along with the attendance at Disneyland.

"Okay, Angie, you stand over there and let me know when the light comes on." I climbed under and over towns and riverbeds until I stood at the far end of the basement. "In position?"

"Ready."

"How about now?"

"Nope."

"Now?"

"Nope." We continued in this vein for quite a while, eventually interspersing conversation between the "nows" and "nopes."

"So Angie, do you know what's bothering Marie? Now?" Darn! The loaded question.

"Nope. And nope, I don't, Jack. She seemed a little, uh, testy this morning."

Jack laughed. "Right. Testy like Mount Vesuvius. Now?"

"Nope."

"But that's one of the things I love about Marie: She is passionate about life. Though I have to say I've never seen her passion take this particular form before. Now?"

"Nope."

I was happy to see that Jack seemed unperturbed about the whole incident. Maybe I had blown it out of proportion.

"So, Angie, how's your love life? Now?"

"Nope. Okay, I guess."

"Haven't found Mr. Right yet? Now?"

"Nope, and nope. Besides I'm not really looking for Mr. Right just yet. I think I need to stay solo for a while, explore a little. Keep my options open."

"Well, love rarely paces itself to come at the perfect time, Angie. It can't be scheduled like trains. Now?"

"Nope. But can't you at least time love so that it doesn't derail you?"

Jack laughed again. "Train analogies, Angie? I think I've made a convert! But even I don't confuse model trains with life. If a train gets derailed, that's it. But people are wired with the capacity to recover from the most catastrophic collisions. Now?"

"Nope. Wait! Yes, yes, the little light is on!" Flushed with our success, Jack flipped the switch sending the entire display into motion. Tiny trains clicked along their tracks; miniature railroad crossing bars fell and lifted in perfect coordination. We stood watching in companionable silence. If only life could click along so smoothly . . .

~~Break in tennies~~

~~Go visit~~ =CALL Gwen after dinner

~~Do Something Nice For CALL Marie tomorrow~~

~~Take a LONG SHORT nap~~

~~Look in Bon Apetit for new recipes for dinner old~~
  ~~Coq Au Vin recipe~~

Make Quick & Easy Garlic Chicken from
  Good Housekeeping

✓ Buy groceries

✓ Meet Jess for Lunch

~~Buy new~~ Iron outfit for brunch with Tim

Tell Jessica to rent Harold and Maude ~~for Jessica~~

Chapter 4

Saturday was not going well so far. My To-Do list was expanding faster than Oprah's waistline (No, wait! Is she in one of her skinny periods again?), with many more revisions than completions. And between Gwen's hysteria, Marie's temper tantrum, Jessica's Tantric twitches, and my own lack of sleep, I was exhausted. But surely the day would improve because Jenna was coming over for dinner.

My daughter entered the world twenty-two years ago as a breath of fresh air that had never grown stale. You never quite knew what Jenna would say or what unusual new friends she might have found or what extraordinary color her hair would be this week (she had been in her Blue Phase, just like Picasso, for the past several months). A constant surprise and a constant delight, Jenna is, as her grandmother always says, a real pistol.

Having Jenna over for dinner was doubly fun because I thoroughly enjoyed cooking again. During my harried-

and-married-working-mom phase, cooking definitely lost its thrill. I had been the frazzled short-order cook at the Picky Eaters' Café. Bob pouted if his food was not breaded and deep-fried. Tyler looked askance at anything related to a tree, bush, or root. For several years, Jenna experimented with various forms of vegetarianism: Ovo, Lacto, Lacto-ovo, Pesco, Pollo, and Peanut Buttero. At a certain point, the only dish the family had in common was strawberry Pop Tarts, which belong to no food group known to man.

But in my newly single state, I could relax and get creative, cooking just for myself and other adults who don't respond with "Eiyou, gross!" whenever an unfamiliar dish is presented. I'd just learned to make my own pasta noodles by hand (the ratio of eating time to cooking time of homemade pasta is about one to one thousand), now shunned cake mixes for pastries from scratch, and explored unusual ways to use exotic ingredients. Have you ever tried stewed, puréed jicama over pumpkin sorbet? Arugula and eggplant salsa? (Actually, don't bother; even Spud and Alli howled "Eiyou, gross!" when I made those.)

That night's challenge was to conquer boiled icing. (Yes, yes, I know that *conquer boiled icing* was not on my To-Do list. But sometimes you have to walk on the wild side, know what I mean?). Boiled icing requires eons of stirring over a double boiler, which is arguably the most boring task in the universe. However, I figured out that I could stand on my step stool and do calf raises while stirring (jumping jacks proved to be a bit too dangerous). So I was perched on my stool, stirring (icing) and sculpting (calves), when Jenna flew through the front door.

"Mom! I've got wonderful news! I'm getting married!"

What ever happened to "Mom, are you sitting down?" I'm quite sure Emily Post insists that *"When announcing exceedingly good news or something shocking, one should always ask if the recipient of said exceedingly good or shocking news is seated."* Perhaps if I had included this training in Jenna's upbringing, I would not have landed on my rear end in the middle of the boiled icing. An icing that I flipped onto the floor after spinning around suddenly on my step stool. A step stool which, as it turns out, though excellent for calf raises was not meant for spinning.

"Mom! Are you okay?"

"I'm fine, sweetie. I don't think I've broken anything. Just help me up." The boiled icing, of course, decided to set up at that precise moment and acted like Super Glue, pasting my pants firmly to the floor. (3M might want to look into the properties of egg whites and liquefied sugar.) Fortunately, Jenna is strong and, working with farm animals, I'm sure she's pulled much heavier critters out of much gooier stuff (though I'd guess this was her first experience yanking a critter out of dessert topping).

Jenna hauled me up, and we shared a sticky hug, which probably lasted a bit longer than usual because of the boiled icing bond we shared in that moment. Spud and Alli enthusiastically plunged into the cleanup efforts at our feet. (In case you are wondering, it turns out beagles love boiled icing.)

"Sweetie, this is wonderful news! When did it all happen? Tell me everything." I pulled off my sticky pants in the bathroom to change and washed the gluey mess off my legs before my thighs bonded permanently as one. My pants had stiffened up completely and stood at attention near the shower. Maybe I could use them as a planter.

"Oh, Mom, it was so romantic! Ryan and I had just finished delivering a calf. It was a difficult birth, and I had to reach in to turn the calf around. Then Ryan grabbed me around the waist to help pull. And when the calf came through, all three of us fell back into the straw in a heap. So there we were, the calf was bleating, Ryan was laughing, and I was crying. Birth is so incredible, Mom! All three of us were muddy and bloody and covered with straw. Ryan turned to me and said we needed to share more moments like this and asked if I would marry him . . ." Okay, so one woman's most romantic moment might inspire another to grab for an airsickness bag. Jenna's face glowed, framed by her sparkling peacock blue hair. She looked so beautiful, so happy, and so very, very young.

"Sweetie, how beautiful! That's a story you'll always remember." And hopefully won't retell during family meals. "But Jenna, are you sure about this? You've only known him for a few months."

"Oh, Mom, of course I'm not sure! Who can ever be sure about anything? But I know I love him. I know he makes me laugh, and we love our work together. Life's an adventure, Mom. Don't we have to grasp it to the fullest?"

Where did this wonderful young woman, with her natural fearlessness and self-confidence, spring from? Had I ever approached life as an adventure? If so, I can't remember it. I remember just taking the next logical step, following my To-Do lists, rarely questioning or looking for unusual options. It's only in the last six months that I had jumped off any cliffs (and actually, I'd been pushed off rather than taking the plunge freely). My first leap into the great unknown had landed me in more hot water than I'd ever been in my life. Now, after substantial damage control, I can't say that I regretted it. So maybe I'd be willing to try a leap, or at least a little hop, in the future.

"You're absolutely right, sweetie. *'Carpe diem!'* And Ryan seems like a wonderful man."

"Oh, Mom, he is! He's so kind with animals and he is serious about his work but can laugh at himself. I love the way he . . ."

Jenna continued to extol Ryan's virtues: his strong hands, good manners, patience with children, wonderful taste in music, great kissing skills. She stopped herself just before waxing eloquent about his sexual prowess. We seem to have a silent mother-daughter understanding about how far that type of conversation goes. I know that Jenna is sexually active. She knows that I know that she is sexually active. But the general knowing is different than the detailed knowing, if you know what I mean. Except for those initial lectures I gave her about safe sex (and the subsequent, much more knowledgeable lectures on the same subject she had given me recently), we approach the subject only in the broadest terms.

"So, sweetie, have you set a date? Talked about what kind of wedding you want?"

"No set date yet, though we think early next year after I'm back in grad school. But I have a scathingly brilliant idea for the wedding!"

Uh-oh. I took a deep breath. Jenna's prior scathingly brilliant ideas had included an excursion to the zoo at age seven to release all of the "poor, caged-up animals." (Luckily, a guard had spied her trying to wriggle her tiny body through the bars of the lions' cage.) At age thirteen, she led a protest against cigarette manufacturers for advertising to teenage smokers. (Fortunately, the fire department arrived before the eight foot Joe Camel effigy she had set on fire could inflame the entire cafeteria of Winston Churchill Middle School.) I shuddered to think what her brilliant idea for this wedding might be and which Sacramento County emergency crews should be alerted. I quickly neutralized my face: If I have three fours, a jack of clubs and . . .

"Mom, I've decided that I want the aunties to be my bridesmaids, and I want you to be matron of honor." The aunties were Gwen, Marie, and Jessica; I think it would be an incredible stretch to call them maids of any kind.

"That's very sweet, Jenna, but highly unusual, isn't it?"

Her face clearly said "and your point is?" Everything about Jenna is highly unusual. She likes it that way, and, honestly, I like it that way, too. Why should her wedding be any different than the rest of her? I was pretty sure that she'd find a role for Spud and Alli in the wedding party as well. (Is there a crash obedience course for aging beagles with adolescent attitudes?)

"Mom, I love the aunties and feel so very close to them. And I don't think it's fair that the mother of the bride gets stuck sitting in the audience. I want you up front with me."

Jenna's eyes glowed with the sweet image of us all

standing beside her on her wedding day. My image was of me blubbering, nose red and swollen from sniffling, with ugly black mascara streaks running down my cheeks. I'm guessing this is why the mother of the bride is usually not onstage during the big event. But this would be Jenna's wedding, Jenna's big moment, and she had the right to do it her way.

"The aunties will be thrilled, sweetie. And so am I. What else have you thought about?"

"I don't know. What else is there? Let's check the Net."

Where we used to run to the library, to the smell of old encyclopedias and thin pages of big dictionaries, now we zip onto the Internet. My kids introduced me to the Internet years ago. At first, I was nervous to enter cyberspace by myself, certain I would get lost out there and float off into the void like that scene in *2001, A Space Odyssey.* (To make me feel more secure, Tyler created an icon on my navigation bar, two little ruby slippers that I could click to get home.)

My first solo explorations on the Internet were not without misadventures. Who knew that a Web site titled *Blondes* would be devoted to ladies with colossal bosoms and not shades of hair dye? (The resulting pop-ups inspired Bob to a whole new level of enthusiasm for computer technology.) But I became more skilled over the years, and search engines became more "user friendly" (translation: Now any idiot can use it).

I turned on my laptop and typed "wedding" into the search box. There were only 8,073,235 sites listed.

"Let's narrow the search, Mom. Add 'planning' and see what comes up."

Better. Only 1,080,083 sites to choose from.

"Try that one. The one that says 'wedding checklist.' "

"They want me to enter a date. What date shall we use, sweetie?"

"How about January 20? That's about ten months away."

I entered the date and a checklist of over two hundred tasks popped up. Oh, my gosh! The Mother of all To-Do lists! Our eyes glazed over as we read down the list.

"Mom, this thing says we are four months behind already."

" 'Find an attorney for the prenuptial agreement.' How romantic."

"What does 'wedding insurance' insure exactly? That I won't trip walking down the aisle? That the champagne will keep its bubbles? That Ryan won't run off with the flower girl?"

"They want us to write a job description for each person in the wedding party. Would that be like 'Groom: Marry the Bride'?"

"And I'm supposed to prepare a list of 'critical questions' regarding my wedding dress. What the heck does that mean?"

"I wonder why we need to book a calligrapher. I got an A in penmanship, and my handwriting is perfectly legible."

"Mom, I don't like this site. Let's try another."

We flipped in and out of several sites. Sites about dresses:

"Here's one, sweetie. The sleeves look like butterfly wings. I wonder if you can really lift off in it?"

"Look at that veil! We could use it as mosquito netting after the wedding."

"Jenna, what about this one? It looks like a six-tiered wedding cake with a head poking out the top of it. Do you suppose it's edible?"

"Or what about the Little Bo Peep one? I could train a sheep to follow me up the aisle . . ."

Sites on wedding favors and gifts:

"Oooo! We could get everyone cute little toothbrushes that say 'Ryan and Jenna' on them. Do you suppose they have the matching floss as well?"

"How about those bridesmaids' bikinis? Wouldn't the aunties just love those? They come with a waxing kit."

Jenna and I giggled our way through several sites, much too excited to do any real planning.

We were starved after our intensive and completely unproductive research. Unfortunately, and predictably, I had forgotten all about my semigourmet dinner. The Quick & Easy Garlic Chicken had long since burned up, dried up, and shriveled up, making itself unrecognizable. We ordered pizza.

"So, Mom," Jenna said through a mouthful of triple cheese and sausage. "I've never heard you talk about your own wedding."

"Oh, it was pretty simple. Your dad and I eloped."

"Eloped? Oh, how romantic!"

Well, truth be known it was not particularly romantic. We eloped because Bob had been afraid to tell his mother that we were getting married, preferring to present our marriage as a fait accompli. And under the circumstances, which we'd never discussed with the kids, we just wanted to do it quickly.

49

"Hmmm. I'd say memorable rather than romantic."

Bob and I were married in Reno at the Chapel O' Love which, for a slight additional charge, offered to repair the crack in Bob's windshield while the ceremony took place. The "chapel," like most of Reno at that time, was decorated in plastic and neon: plastic flowers, plastic ribbons on plastic pews, plastic wedding guests (life-sized blowup dolls, all of whom looked suspiciously like Elvis) and pink neon-lit strips along the sides of the aisle like those emergency strips in airplanes (probably to keep overly inebriated couples on the runway). A weary-looking clerk took our information and our money. We opted for the *With This Ring I Thee Wed* package rather than the cheaper *Dearly Beloved* or more expensive *'Til Death Do Us Part* package. *With This Ring I Thee Wed* guaranteed us at least six and a half minutes of quality vowing time. The clerk handed us a number, lucky number thirty-four, and signaled for us to wait our turn with the other couples in the lobby.

"Number thirty-four!" the elderly lady at the chapel doors hollered. "Here, hon," she said, handing me a fresh bouquet of plastic flowers. "Don't forget to deposit these in the basket by the exit or there's an additional charge of $4.95. Now start down the aisle as soon as you hear your special music." She turned to work the jukebox behind the doors. Apparently our chosen "special music" selection (E17, Pachelbel's Canon in D) looked just like F17 to her. We ended up walking down the aisle to "Muskrat Love."

Then there was The Toupee.

The minister, ordained through the Poughkeepsie Mail-Order School of Divinity and Auto Repair, had a bushy black vinyl toupee precariously perched just left of center on his scalp. With each pronouncement and each solemn head nod, his plastic hairpiece would shift ever so slightly to the west. Bob and I stood at the altar, mesmerized at the movement of The Toupee.

"Dearly Beloved . . ." *shift.*

"If there be anyone present who knows why this man and this woman . . ." *shift.*

"And, do you . . . I'm sorry, what is your name, hon? Angela? Angela, do you take this man . . ." *shift.*

"I now pronounce you man and wife!" *Plop!* The toupee fell directly onto my bouquet of plastic peonies and gladiolas.

After my blow-by-blow description of the whole event, Jenna and I rolled around on the floor, laughing uncontrollably and clutching our aching stomachs. Her dad and I had done exactly the same thing as we exited the Chapel O' Love.

"All right, Mom," Jenna said, wiping tears from her eyes. "So now I know why I'm so weird. But weren't you disappointed that it wasn't more . . . I don't know, romantic? Beautiful?"

"Oh, not really, sweetie. I've been behind the scenes of some really beautiful weddings. And let me tell you, it can get pretty ugly back there. Seems to bring out the worst in some people."

Traditionally, the stress of putting on a wedding is second only to the pressure of orchestrating the Academy Awards. Perfectly nice people become vain, self-centered, petty, and strongly opinionated about things they never cared about before: who wears what shoes, which little almond things go into what kind of little net baggies, who sits next to whom, candles or flowers, sit-down or buffet. The easiest wedding I remember was the one where the bride and her mother shared their Valium with the entire wedding party. The worst one required a small contingent of the National Guard to separate warring soon-to-be in-laws.

Marriage itself is rarely as traumatic as the wedding. What's that old saying? "If boot camp is difficult, then the war will be easy." Maybe that's the point of stressful weddings: If the bride and groom can survive it, the marriage itself will be a walk in the park (not Central Park, of course, but one of those safer, small-town parks with no professional muggers on active duty).

"But we're not like other people, are we, Mom? We don't have to get all crazy over a little old wedding, do we? And as you always said, it's about the marriage, not about the wedding. Right?"

"I said that?"

"I think so. It was either you or Mr. Rogers."

Jenna left after a little while, taking her new bride-to-be glow with her, leaving my mother-of-the-bride glow with me. I got ready for bed, my boiled-icing pants still standing guard in the bathroom. Maybe they would come in handy as an extra towel rack.

For the second night in a row, I could not fall asleep, but this time it was out of excitement. How do the years fly by so quickly? One minute, I'm holding my beautiful baby girl in my arms, tears running down my cheeks, and in the next minute I'm hugging the lovely woman she has become, the same tears running down slightly more wrinkled cheeks. And maybe someday soon I would have a grand-child to hold. A grandchild! Forty-nine is definitely not too young to be a grandmother. My cousin Annette is exactly my age and she has a gaggle of them. Not that it's a com-petition, but if Jenna and Ryan could . . .

But first things first. The wedding itself was the next step. And even though Jenna clearly had her feet on the ground about this wedding, there was still a lot to plan. Would it really be in January? A rainy month around here, but the holiday rush will be over, and it will be easier to find churches and reception halls. What will she wear? For my own wedding, I had opted for jeans with lace around the cuffs and a white embroidered shirt (by Chapel O' Love standards, this was pretty dressy.) But Jenna has an un-usual and exquisite sense of style, so who knows what she'll want?

And I need to get to know Ryan better. I wonder what his parents are like. And his groomsmen, will they all be much younger than the aunties? Will we look like a pro-cession from a Mothers and Sons Dance walking down the aisle? What about those little almond candies? Jenna hates almonds. Couldn't we substitute M&Ms? The pastel ones, not those bright blue ones. Though the bright blue ones do match Jenna's hair . . .

My mind wandered aimlessly until I finally fell asleep, my clock reading 2:47 A.M., secure in the knowledge that no matter what Jenna decided, my daughter would be one of the rare brides who does not get crazy or go overboard on her wedding preparations.

And yes, to answer your unspoken question, I can be incredibly naïve.

~~Go visit~~=CALL Gwen ~~after dinner~~ TOMORROW

~~Do Something Nice For~~ CALL Marie ~~tomorrow~~

~~Take a LONG~~ SHORT ~~nap~~

~~Look in Bon Apetit for new recipes for dinner~~

   ~~Coq Au Vin recipe~~

✓ ~~Make Quick & Easy Garlic Chicken from~~

   ~~Good Housekeeping~~

✓ Order pizza for dinner

✓ Buy groceries

✓ Meet Jess for Lunch

~~Break in tennies~~

~~Buy new~~ Iron outfit for brunch with Tim

Tell Jessica to rent <u>Harold and Maude</u> ~~for Jessica~~

Buy wedding magazines!

Test wedding candies! (do Jelly Bellies come

   in pastels?)

Tighten tummy and lose saddlebags for wedding!

Find waterproof mascara for wedding!

Chapter 5

Jenna made a beautiful bride. Her hair was adorned with special sparkles so that it glowed like a peacock blue fairy crown. In fact, to honor the bride, everyone in the wedding party had their dyed hair in fanciful colors: Tyler's was purple, Gwen chose red with a slash of black angled up the front, Jessica's locks were green with bright yellow tips, Marie had selected deep sea blue. Even Bob had dyed his few remaining stray hairs a bright fluorescent orange, combing them carefully over his bald spots. All of the guests in attendance had joined the fun as well, creating a beautiful rainbow sea of heads in the pews. What a wonderful tribute to Jenna! I looked in the mirror. Oh, no! In the rush of getting ready, I must have forgotten my dye. My mousey brown hair looked plain and ugly and out of place. A stern-looking guard came through the crowd and grabbed my elbow. "Ma'am, I'm afraid you'll have to leave." "But . . . but, I'm the bride's mother." "Jenna wouldn't have a mother who is so ordinary, so boring. Please come with me, ma'am." He touched a button on his belt that set off a shrill alarm. Brrrng! Brrrng! "No! I *can't go! That's my baby getting married!"* Brrrng! Brrrng! I *struggled against his grasp* to pick up the phone. The clock said 6:15.

"Angie, wake up for heavens sakes! Our girl is getting married! How can you be sleeping at a time like this?" The chirpy Southern drawl assaulting my sleep-deprived ears could only be Lilah, my mother-in-law, my ex-mother-in-law if you take into account the divorce, which Lilah does not. She also refuses to take into account that we exist in different time zones.

"I can't believe you're still in bed with all of this excitement, Angie. I swear you could sleep through your own wake!" Isn't that the idea? I can't imagine that guests at my wake would be thrilled to see me leap out of my coffin to do the hully-gully. But I rarely argue with Lilah, especially if I've not been armed with my first cup of coffee.

"I was just getting up, Lilah." I smiled as I imagined her sitting at her kitchen window, eighty-year-old hands bejeweled and sparkling in the sun, slightly pinkish curls topping her tiny five-foot frame. She is the type of little old lady who can wear a shocking gold lamé jumpsuit and make you wish you had one yourself. She can (and often does) say outrageous things. Most people get arrested for those comments; Lilah gets laughs. I hope I'm a lot like Lilah when I hit her age.

"I just wish the wedding didn't have to be in Sacramento. Couldn't it be in California somewhere?"

"Uh, Lilah, Sacramento is in California."

"No, no, no! I mean in the *real* California, like San Francisco or LA. Someplace with charm and character. Sacramento should be in Iowa or Kansas. It's so ordinary! The only reason anyone visits Sacramento is to get hay fever."

She had a point, one that we Sacramentens stubbornly ignore. We don't have the chic, exotic aura of San Francisco, the pulsing drive of Silicon Valley, or the glitz of LA. Mostly we brag about Sacramento as being "close" to everything: close to Wine Country, close to the City (Please! You set our teeth on edge when you call it 'Frisco!), close to Lake Tahoe. And I'm pretty sure we have the lock on Allergy Capital of the Nation. I've heard that Sacramento is second only to Paris in the number and variety of trees it has. Maybe we're lacking the Champs Elysées and the Louvre, but if you've never experienced the thrill of hay fever, come to Sacramento and bring plenty of tissue.

Of course, Tyler claims that Sacramento is the Capital of the Universe. He was ten years old when he developed this hypothesis:

"See, Mom, it's the capital of the state that has the biggest economy in the nation that has the biggest economy in the world. And since we don't know if there is life on other planets, well, that covers the universe as well."

Good theory, huh? But I have to agree with Lilah; Sacramento ranks pretty high on the boring scale. It's unlikely that we'll see *Sex in Sacramento* or *Sacramento Confidential* as hit TV shows. But then again, Lilah lives in Macon, Georgia. How exciting can that be?

The other thing about Sacramento is that everyone is connected to everyone. That Kevin Bacon thing of six degress of separation? If you're from Sacramento, you have three degrees *max* to connecting with anyone else from Sacramento. I am not exaggerating. In my newly single state, it's occurred to me that a quick fling with a stranger from Sacramento is totally out of the question. It would take less than five minutes to establish that the guy went to kindergarten with the cousin of one of my neighbors. Not that I am interested in a quick fling with a stranger; I'm just saying if I was, I couldn't get away with it.

Lilah was still speaking as my drowsy, dopey brain considered all of this.

"So what do you think of the groom, Angie? A little old for Jenna, don't you think? Closer to your age than hers." I hadn't done the math yet. Let's see, forty-nine (me) minus thirty-seven (him) equals twelve. Thirty-seven (him) minus twenty-two (Jenna) equals, uh, somewhat more than twelve. I really needed that cup of coffee. "But then a lot of old codgers like younger women. Look at Tony Randall and that Heather somebody. Did you know that she was fifty years younger than he was? He became a father at seventy, silly man. Who wants to change diapers on the way to pick up your Social Security check? That's probably what killed him. A really nasty dirty diaper," she concluded decisively.

"Lilah, I'm don't think Ryan can be classified as an old codger at thirty-seven. He probably has a few good years left in him, and he and Jenna seem very compatible." I pulled my sleepy body parts out of bed in search for the caffeinated Holy Grail.

"I suppose you're right, Angie. And who knows what attracts people to each other? Look at Tyler and that Cyndee.

Who would have guessed that my brilliant grandson would hook up with a woman with the brain of a salamander. And what's up with the 'ee'?"

"The what?"

"You know, spelling Cyndee with an 'ee' rather than a 'y.' Makes her sound like a candy bar or a *Penthouse* centerfold. Of course, the ones that end with 'i' sound worse, like a dot com or something. What ever happened to the good old 'y'?"

"Hmmm. I don't know, Lilah." I stumbled toward my kitchen, tripping over Alli, my dot com beagle, and started some coffee. Like getting stuck with an obnoxious tune in my head, I was sure my brain would be filled with ee's, i's, and "What ever happened to the 'y'?" for the rest of the day.

"Of course, those hooters of hers look like the Rocky Mountains. Do you think they're real? Have you gotten a good look at them?" Oh goody! So maybe I'd be stuck contemplating the possible artificiality of Cyndee's breasts all day instead: Does she or doesn't she . . . ?

"Gosh, not really, Lilah." I managed to get the coffee brewing and felt a glimmer of hope.

"Well, those hooters alone could explain it. But what about Bob and that woman? How do you explain that?"

Bob, my ex, is Lilah's son, and "that woman" is Lilah's not so endearing nickname for Clarisse. Ever since Bob left me for Clarisse, Lilah has made a point of boycotting Clarisse's actual name and calling her "that woman." I choose to believe that I am not spiteful (don't we all?), but I get a definite, smug little thrill every time Lilah says it: "that woman." Ha!

"Must be chemistry, Lilah."

"Oh, don't be so naïve, Angie! It was cash, not chemistry. That woman is loaded, and Bob is living like a geriatric gigolo."

I know better than to laugh out loud at Lilah's cracks about Bob. I've seen her draw blood defending her Baby Boy. "Uh, I think Bob's a little young to be considered 'geriatric.'"

"Don't be so literal, my dear. By the way, how is your love life coming along?"

It's a good thing I'd managed to produce that cup of coffee because these postdivorce conversations with Lilah get tricky. We share stories like old girlfriends, but after all, she is my mother-in-law, so I try to be delicate and circumspect.

"Well, let's see. I'm still seeing Tim."

"Mr. Music Store? With the great smile and perky buns?" Clearly, Lilah didn't share my need for delicacy.

"How would you know about his, uh, posterior?"

"Thanksgiving. I met all of the candidates. Tim, that slightly dour attorney from Tyler's office . . ."

"Eric? He's still in the mix."

"And what about that delightful pediatrician, Jonathan? I do think he took a fancy to me that evening, Angie. But since he is geographically undesirable as far as I'm concerned, I release him to you."

"Gosh, thanks, Lilah."

"So have you done the dirty with any of them yet?"

I spewed my mouthful of coffee all over the kitchen floor. "Done the what?" I sputtered, choking.

"You know, put the wiener in the bun, slapped the sword in the scabbard, shucked the corn cob with the . . ."

"Um, I'm taking it slow on that score, Lilah."

Actually, Tim and I came pretty close after a Rod Stewart concert one night. I didn't think I remembered much of Rod Stewart. But the first chords of "Maggie May" pulled every single lyric of every one of his songs out of some deep, dingy corner in my brain (that same corner where the last three digits of my license plate number remain permanently captive). Think this wouldn't happen to you? Hum a few bars of "You're in My Heart, You're in My Soul" and see.

In the second half of the show, Rod sang the real oldies, not the oldies from when we were youngies but the oldies that my parents had listened to: "It Had to Be You," "The Very Thought of You," etc., the truly romantic stuff.

By the final chorus of "Bewitched, Bothered and Bewildered," Tim and I were feeling pretty amorous. In the parking lot, we did a very good job of steaming up his car windows. But at the moment of truth (when we would have found out whether we were still agile enough to "perform" in the backseat of his car), the alarm of the SUV next to us erupted. Eleven security guards surrounded us, like G-men ready to take on Bonnie and Clyde. So the moment of truth passed and by the time we stood at my front door my caution had returned.

"Tim," I had said, as he moved his arm around me. "Uh, I think we'd better stop here."

"Are you sure?" his lips were nuzzling my neck, right under my left ear. The killer spot.

"Uh, yes. I'm, um, just not ready."

"Hmmm. You seemed pretty ready back in the parking lot at Arco Arena."

"Tim!" I pushed him away before the nuzzling got further into the danger zone. "I'm maybe physically ready. But I'm just not *ready* ready."

"I'm sorry, Angie." He gave me his "aw, shucks" smile, which was almost as lethal as his neck nuzzling. "I guess maybe it's too soon since your divorce?"

"Well, that and this is only our third date." I didn't bother to mention that my very first date with someone else had ended up in bed, a terrible mistake I didn't want to repeat and a story I didn't think Tim needed to know.

"Third? I count four."

"Thanksgiving doesn't count. That was a family gathering, not a date."

"And there were a couple of other guys there, right? Guys you might be interested in." Tim's face had gone blank.

"No, uh, yes. Um, I don't really know yet. I just feel like I shouldn't rush into anything. That I should keep my options open and explore, at least for a while." Tim looked at me silently, and I had wondered if I was making another terrible mistake, this time on the side of too much caution. "Tim, I just don't think I could be with you and feel comfortable even exploring."

"You mean 'be with me' in the Biblical sense?"

"Uh, yeah."

"But it's a possibility at some point?"

"Definitely." I'm sure I was blushing to my toenails.

"I like the sound of that." He smiled. "I can be patient." And he kissed me again. Heck, I'm glad he can be patient because I'm not sure I can.

Lilah's voice, which had been trilling nonstop during my reverie, finally snapped me back to the present.

"Angie dear, are you all right? Did I just hear you moan?"

"Uh, no, I don't think so. Coffee was just a little too hot."

"Well, I'm just saying don't wait too long to hit the sheets, my dear. Use it or lose it, as they say. And remember: As your beaus get older and start wearing pacemakers, you can't let them get too close to your electric pleasure toys. Some of the battery-operated ones are okay . . ."

"Lilah, I promise that when I get to that point I'll call and check out the logistics with you."

"You do that. Now, about the wedding. You've got a lot to do if they're planning for early next year. Mother of the Bride is a big job, Angie. And, if you don't mind me being indelicate, my dear, how do you intend to pay for it?"

This time I gulped rather than spewed my coffee. It remained lodged uncomfortably in my throat. The "pay for it" part of Jenna's nuptials hadn't hit me yet. I wasn't quite sure how much a wedding would cost, but I figured it must be somewhere between a new sofa bed and a chateau on the Seine, neither of which I could afford.

Our financial situation since the divorce was relatively simple. Bob, through his "association" with Clarisse, had lots of money. I had none. Oh, I had enough to live on; I make fairly good money working as an asset manager for a local developer, and my living expenses are minimal. But all of my savings had been wiped out by the divorce. I still had a tiny bit in an IRA, but don't they report you to Homeland Security and cut off your toes if you make early withdrawals from those accounts? This would take some heavy-duty, intensive thinking, not a good activity on less than four hours of sleep.

"Angie, dear, maybe I could help." Lilah, through a shrewd choice of extremely well heeled husbands and extremely ferocious divorce attorneys, had become very wealthy herself. She was generous with her money, especially to her only child, Bob. Through the years of our marriage, she even continued to pay Bob a monthly stipend, a practice that made me cringe. (However, she had cut off Bob's allowance after he moved in with "that woman," muttering something about not bankrolling wayward zippers. Ha! Honestly, I am *not* a spiteful person.)

She was equally generous with me and with the kids; Jenna and Tyler grew up thinking Santa had unlimited credit at FAO Schwarz. I know Lilah enjoyed the giving, and perhaps she was trying to make up for the grandparental gap my parents had left, dying as they did before the kids were old enough to know them. But sometimes her largesse made me uncomfortable. How do you ever repay generosity like hers?

"Thank you for the offer, Lilah. I really do appreciate it. But we've got some time, so let's play it by ear, figure out how much it's going to cost, and see what happens." Maybe Donald Trump had a little extra lying around that he'd be willing to donate . . .

A New Day, a New List:
  Break in Tennies
  Call Gwen

Ask Jess re: incantations for winning Lottery
Iron brunch outfit
Take a LONG, LONG nap
Dinner Tyler & Cyndee ~~(check out hooters)~~
Figure out budget for wedding

Still in my jammies, I started at the bottom of my To-Do list, reentering cyberspace to look up wedding costs and budgeting. The whole issue is about as simple as the national defense budget. (Did you know that they don't typically plug in any money for wars in those defense budgets? I think the theory is that war is some kind of bonus activity, like a kid who earns extra allowance for doing extra chores.) Depending on the overall wedding budget, different percentages are allocated to different aspects of the wedding. For instance, if you spend a million dollars on a wedding, your cake may only be 1 percent of your budget and the jets you hire to fly your wedding guests to your private island may be 5 percent. If you plan to spend a total of five hundred dollars on the wedding, assume it will be potluck (allot 5 percent of the budget for the three-tiered Jell-O mold), and guests will buy their own bus passes to the judge's office.

Fortunately, several sites have budget worksheets. You just plug in a bottom line number and see what happens. I started with $1500; I figured I could give up Starbucks for the next ten months and save that much. Per the Official Wedding Budget Calculator, considering all expenses with gratuities and tax, this gave us $98.17 to spend on Jenna's dress and $5.43 per guest for food; Jenna would be wearing a toga made from a knockoff designer sheet and Burger King would cater the reception. I tried $15,000. The amount allotted to each category looked more reasonable but it still left just $100 each for the wedding rings. Why would you spend more on a gown you'll wear once for a few hours than on a ring you'll hopefully wear for the rest of your life? But the question was moot, because no matter how many lattés and mixed berry scones I sacrificed, I'd never have that kind of money in time. (It must be nice to be the government and have deficit spending as an option when you just can't make the numbers add up.)

I was morosely engrossed in this bleak budget analysis, still in my jammies plugging in numbers and feeling hopeless, when I heard a knock at the door. It was Tim, of course. Ack!

Chapter 6

"Oh, gosh, I'm so sorry, Tim. I completely lost track of time. Give me a few moments to get cleaned up."

"No problem, Angie. But you look fine as is." He grinned. Perhaps Tim is particularly nearsighted.

I did not look fine as is. Besides the fact that I was wearing a flannel nightie that only residents of the Happy Hour Rest Home could find appealing, I am not one of those natural beauties who look great as soon as they leap out of bed. I look more like Phyllis Diller than Phyllis George; my natural beauty takes at least an hour and a half of concentrated effort to put together.

How embarrassing! After months of carefully planning my wardrobe, my hair, my makeup, and my scent for every casual encounter with Tim, I blow it by showing him the real me, natural and unprocessed. Of course, I'd often hoped that eventually Tim might see me as I first wake up in the morning. But that would have been after an evening of, well, enough romance to soften his perception of the bags under my eyes.

Tim was still grinning, rubbing Spud's tummy and Alli's ears, as he watched me scramble nervously through my closet. What was it Jenna had coached me to wear for brunch dates? Ah, the little jeans skirt and a knit shirt (or was it the knit skirt with the jeans shirt?). I grabbed my clothes and shoes, then dumped an entire drawer full of bras and panties as I hurriedly scooped up my underwear. It's not easy to be modest in a studio.

"Um, Tim, make yourself comfortable. I'll be just a minute." He looked over at my unmade bed, the kitchen chairs covered with last night's clothes and today's laundry, the dogs' bed, and finally settled tactfully in the desk chair. Kicking myself for having trashed whatever good first impressions I had made with Tim, I headed to the bathroom.

During my thirty-second shower, I struggled to remember the six steps in *Two Minutes to a Beautiful You!* Are there really women who need just six steps and two minutes to get beautiful? Or is this one of those con jobs like *Learn to Speak Serbo-Croatian in Thirty-two Hours?* We are definitely a microwave culture; everything needs to happen right now or sooner. Could Michelangelo create *David* out of a slab of marble within two minutes and with just six steps? I don't think so. As for me, I was starting with a slab of something more akin to Spam than marble. It might take a bit longer.

Step One: Clean. All orifices, crevices, and surfaces. Check.
Step Two: Shine. Hair, nails, teeth. Check.

Step Three: Camouflage. Blemishes, dark spots, ill-formed bone structure. (Without a hood over my face and garbage bag to cover my body, I could hardly check off that one.) Semicheck.

Step Four: Define. Brows (plucked), lips (lined), bust-line (padded). Check.

Step Five: Color. Cheeks (healthy glow), lips (shining anticipation), eyelids (sultry expectation). Check.

Step Six: Scent. Spritz nape of neck, back of knees, wrists. Check.

When I had dressed and done as much as I could do to turn Spam into *A Beautiful Me!,* I made my grand entrance from the bathroom. Tim was sitting at my desk, staring glassy-eyed at the computer screen. He was no longer smiling.

"I'm sorry I wasn't ready, Tim. But I was engrossed in some research on the computer."

"Hmmm. So I see. You were looking at, uh, wedding sites?" His voice sounded a little strained.

"Yes, Jenna and I spent half the evening looking at these sites, and I got back into it this morning. Can you believe how much information is available? Dresses, flowers, variations of ceremonies. I was just working on a budget."

Tim looked stricken. "So, uh, are you, um . . ."

"Me? Oh, no! It's Jenna. Jenna is getting married. She told me just last night."

"She did?" Tim sounded even more uncomfortable.

"Yes, my little girl! I guess every mother dreams of this moment. It's so very exciting!"

"You do? It is?" He was positively squirming by then. What could be bothering him?

I recalled a tenet from *The Rules,* a militant guide to dating I'd read when I reentered the fray a few months ago. One of *The Rules'* rules (which I had obviously just broken) is that a woman should never, ever, under any circumstances bring up the subject of marriage or weddings no matter what the context. Apparently, studies have shown that the topic of matrimony in any form will bring the average single American male to a state of instant terror, prompting either the fight or flight syndrome or cardiac arrest. From Tim's suddenly pale face, I couldn't tell which I'd set off.

Tim, DWM, has been single for several years. He is attractive (very attractive, actually) with no obvious character defects, excellent personal hygiene, and a killer smile. So why was he still available? Maybe he is one of those commitment-phobic males who would choose death over any kind of relationship. Poor guy! He probably thought I was trying to snare him (though my flannel nightie should have told him that my intention was not seduction). I tried to wriggle out of my blunder.

"Uh, no. I mean, yes, of course. It's exciting for *her.* Personally, I am not at all interested in marriage. For myself that is."

"You aren't?" Tim, if anything, looked even more discomfited. Oh, heck! What had I said wrong now? These treacherous waters of dating definitely required more brainpower than I could muster on my three and a half hours of sleep. We rode to brunch in uncomfortable silence.

You know, this dating thing is not as fun and easy as I remembered it from thirty years ago. My postdivorce dating experience has been limited: one memorably catastrophic one-night stand, a couple of blind dates (I'm convinced that the purpose of a blind date is to make you grateful for the power of sight), a few dates with Tim and some almost-dates with a couple of others. But preparation for even this little bit of dating activity had been hard work, as time-consuming as an extra part-time job.

For instance, I'd had to drastically alter my wardrobe. According to my dating advisors (Gwen, Marie, Jessica, and Jenna), my working soccer mom outfits were unsatisfactory. My new fashion statement was supposed to be "available but not easy," a far departure from "don't mind me, I'm just the mom." So gradually my baggy khakis were being replaced with slim-fitting capris, business suits augmented with feminine dresses, practical navy blues and grays supplanted by bright colors according to my "season." Being a summer/spring, I was strictly forbidden from wearing winter or—God forbid!—autumn colors. (I'm not exactly sure what happens if you wear the wrong season; maybe your leaves fall off?)

I also had to get on a regular regime of leg shaving. For years, I had shaved my legs just once per month in the winter, my own contribution to energy conservation. In the summer, I shaved slightly more often. (Though I've always believed that a light tan adequately camouflages leg hairs that are less than a quarter inch long.) Apparently, for dating purposes, this schedule is simply not acceptable. Then there's the issue of exactly how far up the leg you are supposed to shave. According to some experts, shaving only up to the knee means the date hasn't got a chance, but shaving to midthigh level indicates readiness for a heavy make-out session. Shaving above midthigh signals willingness for activities that might require contraception.

Besides wardrobe and accelerated leg shaving, I had to change my sleeping patterns as well. This was the hardest adjustment of all. Normally, though not recently, I get up by 5:00 A.M. and hit the sack by 8:30 P.M. This schedule was perfect for raising kids, especially when they were small. But we singles are supposed to do our swinging in the late-night hours. I wonder why? I suppose there are some practical arguments for it (e.g., most of us look better in moonlight or candlelight or no light at all). But couldn't some of us morning people date on a swing shift schedule? Hit the matinees and the early-bird dinner specials?

And dating itself? What's it really all about anyway? Two people come together trying to get to know each other, each putting only his/her best foot forward while desperately trying to expose the other person's hidden foot. As a vehicle for discovering the true nature of a person, a date is about as revealing as the essay portion of the Miss America pageant.

In my opinion if you really want to get to know someone and test for compatibility, go out and buy a sofa together. All will be revealed.

"You think *pink* is a neutral color?"

"Dog hairs? You let your *dogs* on the sofa?"

"No leather? You're a vegetarian? Does that mean no leopardskin either?"

"Doilies? On the armrests?"

"How big? Really? So how often does your whole family visit anyway?"

"Why do I need to know if it's long enough for me to sleep on? By myself?"

"Scotchguard? You're not planning to eat on the sofa, are you?"

"Pocket for the remote? What do you mean you'll be living here during football season?"

See what I mean? One sofa date could be very effective, telling you all you need to know about someone without wasting a lot of time and mascara.

Gwen claims that dating is like reading a book. Usually by the first page, you'll know if you want to abandon the book and not read it at all. But you can't tell by the first page or even the first chapter whether you'll enjoy the book all the way through. I was on about page fifteen with Tim, really liked what I'd read so far, but who knew if I'd make it through to the end? And besides, I was keeping my romantic options open, remember?

Dating Tim was usually a mixture of exciting and comfortable. Sometimes I'd feel so at ease with him that I'd forget that we were even on a date. But then he'd touch my hand, and all sorts of sparks would fly up my spine, in my stomach, and other parts of my anatomy. It was everything I could do to maintain my vow of temporary celibacy.

But this particular date was unusually awkward and tense. Tim didn't touch my hand, didn't talk, didn't even

smile or look at me. I know I had blundered with that wedding reference, but hadn't I repaired the damage? Finally, I
pulled out the Magic Question, the inquiry guaranteed to
get an eloquent response from any breathing male (and a
few who have ceased to breathe). Cleopatra used it to en-
tice Mark Antony, Daisy Mae breathed it into Li'l Abner's
ear, and each of Henry VIII's wives used it successfully on
the king (before they were beheaded, of course). To my
knowledge, the Magic Question has never failed in the his-
tory of male/female communication:

"So, Tim, how's work?"

"I don't know, Angie. It's getting rougher and rougher
these days." (Tim's floodgates were open. See how easy
that was?) "Small entrepreneurs in every industry are getting gobbled up by big conglomerates or crushed trying to
compete with them. The music business is in the same
struggle." Tim, along with a couple of silent partners,
owned four or five record stores throughout California
and Nevada. (Of course, these record stores didn't actually
sell any records, only CDs and tapes. But why bother re-
naming them as "CD and Tapes" stores? The next techno-
logical innovation is sure to hit as soon as new stationary
is printed and the new neon sign is installed.) "The stores
are still doing well, but as the guy in charge, I'm the one
responsible for making sure they continue to do so. And
I'm tired of the effort and the travel, the pressure, the
whole thing."

"So what will you do?" The nice thing about the Magic
Question is that once it primes a man's pump, there's not
very much more you need to contribute.

"I've talked to a couple of the partners, and they may be willing to buy me out. Or there's a chain out of New Jersey that might . . ." My attention started to fade as he got into mind-numbing details. Sometimes the pump gets overly primed.

"So if you sell the business, Tim, what will you do next?" We were in the restaurant, the last fifteen miles of the drive a steady stream of equity positions, partner concerns, buy-out strategies, and tax considerations. Not that I wasn't interested, but listening to Tim's monologue could beat out benzodiazepine as a sleep aid. I wonder if I could tape him . . . ?

"Well, I'd be set up pretty well financially. I was thinking of just traveling around for a few months. When I traveled for the business, all I ever saw were airports and the inside of hotel rooms. I'm nearly fifty; I want to spend some time seeing more of the world than I've seen so far."

"So, are you thinking maybe one of those cross-country Harley trips?"

Tim laughed and gave me one of his delectable grins. "No, Angie, I'm afraid that would be a little too rough on my, uh, my kidneys." He reached over and put his warm hand over mine. See? All this progress from the Magic Question! "And I've been thinking that I wouldn't want to travel all alone."

"Would you take one of the boys?" Tim has four children, all grown; girls married, boys not.

"Actually, Angie, I was thinking . . ."

Brrrng! Brrng! My purse started ringing loudly, jumping around the table like a prop in *The Exorcist*. "Sorry, Tim. Just a minute. Hello? Oh, Gwen, I meant to call you . . . You can't figure out . . . ? You want my opinion on . . . ? Well, I'd say the taupe . . . Yes . . . Okay . . ." I sat dumbfounded at the end of the call.

"What was that?"

"Uh, Gwen. She wanted my advice on what shoes to wear, can you believe it?" Tim looked at me quizzically. Of course not knowing Gwen, he couldn't appreciate how bizarre an event it was. Gwen *never* asks for my opinion or anyone else's. She's usually as decisive as a Major League umpire at home plate, and as adamantly opinionated as a WRONG WAY sign. But this was not the time to figure out what was wrong with Gwen. Tim was looking restless again.

"Never mind. You were saying, Tim?"

He had retracted his hand and was studying the menu. "Nothing important."

By the time we ordered, it was apparent that Tim and I were back to square one. Of course, I could have pulled out Magic Question Number Two: "How about those '49'ers/Lakers/Blue Jays?" The problem with Magic Question Number Two is that it's like Bermuda grass choking out the rest of the lawn. Once introduced, no other topic of conversation will ever break through. Besides, with my sleep tank registering just below E, I couldn't quite remember which sports season we were in.

Fortunately, with men of a certain age, there is Magic Question Number Three:

"So, Tim, how are your grandkids?"

This time Tim's face lit up so deliciously that I was ready

to throw all of my underwear at him with me still in it. "Little Maggie is so cute! I've got a picture." He pulled out two pictures: The first showed Tim playing airplane with Maggie, holding her high above his head. The second was taken four seconds later when Maggie had tossed her cookies, her breakfast actually, all over him. Tim's smile never faded from picture to picture.

"Tim, I've got to say this is my favorite picture of you."

"Why? Because someone just barfed on me?"

"No, because . . ." Brrng! Brrng! "Oh, heck, I'm sorry, Tim. I'm waiting for a phone call from , uh, someone." Actually, Jenna had said that her soon-to-be in-laws might call. But I couldn't say that to Tim; it would bring up the dreaded topic of wedding again. "Hello? So, what's up, Jess? . . . You did what? . . . So then . . . ? But if . . ." Jessica spoke nonstop, mostly about subjects that have been banned in the Bible Belt, taking no breaths at all for the next five minutes. I shrugged my apologies to Tim who was by then staring out the window. Finally, I got a word in edgewise and ended the call. "Tim, that was so rude. I never do that. I'm so sorry."

"That's okay, Angie." His voice didn't sound as if it was okay. "Shall we go?"

We drove home in uncomfortable silence, with no more Magic Questions to bring us back together.

~~Break in Tennies~~
~~Call Gwen~~
~~Ask Jess re: incantations for winning Lottery~~

HEATHER ESTAY

Take a ~~LONG~~ short nap
~~Iron brunch outfit~~
Dinner Tyler & Cyndee ~~(check out hooters)~~
~~Figure out budget~~ Create miracle to pay for wedding
Take Tim sofa shopping?

Chapter 7

Usually, I look forward to evenings with Tyler. We have an easy rapport, and I love the young man he has become as much as I ever loved the delightful child he had been. But the dynamics had changed now that all of our gatherings included Cyndee.

It's not that I really mind Cyndee. Except that she always monopolizes the conversation, and she talks in exclamation points like that old comic strip *Brenda Starr,* and she flirts with every waiter and busboy within range, and she clings to Tyler's side like a rash . . . okay, so Cyndee with the ee was definitely starting to get on my nerves, and I don't think spelling her name with a y would have helped much.

My cardinal rule is never, ever to criticize the spouse or significant other of family members or friends. (This was especially good policy when the kids were teenagers and determined to act in polar opposition to my excellent advice.) As time moves on, what if that the "impossible jerk" becomes a lifer, showing up for thirty years of Thanksgiving dinners and Easter egg hunts? Besides, who listens? All three of my best friends disliked Bob from the very beginning and told me so. But it took me twenty-six years to agree with them; their obvious dislike in the interim only made my life miserable.

So I swallowed my irritation and bad attitude and fixed my happy poker face firmly in place to meet Tyler and the ever-present Cyndee at my favorite Chinese restaurant. Cyndee showed up in a *Fredrick of Hollywood* outfit with underwear positioned as outerwear, the look that used to be scandalous on Madonna and is now standard issue for thirteen-year-olds. The men in the restaurant found it too difficult not to gawk at Cyndee, so they went ahead and gawked.

It isn't just Cyndee's clothing that makes her gawkable. She has a body that's perfectly designed to help Victoria sell her Secrets. Being around Cyndee, whose body parts were so perky and curvy, makes me feel especially saggy and unaugmented. Marie had introduced me to the miracle of Miracle bras a few months back; I wear them, but there's only so much miracle in any one bra. Raw material is minimal in my case. But traveling in Cyndee's wake, I figured no one would notice or care.

Being regulars, Tyler and I knew to order quickly when the sour-faced elderly waiter stomped up to our table. This particular Chinese restaurant has great food but the waitstaff makes it very clear that it is a total imposition to serve you. If you don't order immediately when your waiter shows up, you may not get a second chance. The staff will ignore you completely, letting you famish, quarantined at your table while aromatic plates of moo goo gai pan and broccoli beef pass you by. Cyndee, however, didn't know she was at risk of starvation as she batted her eyelashes and tossed her blond locks coquettishly, determinedly trolling for the drooling admiration she usually elicits. She giggled and flirted heroically as our waiter scowled at her, tapping his pencil impatiently and muttering in Mandarin. Cyndee was seriously close to losing her chance to eat.

As entertaining as it was to watch their mutual frustration, I was there to be with my son. I turned to Tyler with Magic Question #1:

"So, honey, how's work going?"

"Oh, he's loving it, Angie!" Cyndee broke in enthusiastically. The way Cyndee pronounced my name it sounded like I had grown some extra ee's of my own. "He wakes up in the morning and literally leaps out of bed! And though he's worn-out at night, he's still excited. Of course he can't tell even *me* what he's working on, but . . ." This young woman was good. In the course of three sentences, she had definitely staked out Tyler as her territory as effectively as peeing a circle around him. She let me know she was with Tyler when he awoke and when he went to bed. Score one for Cyndee. Tyler smiled indulgently. I silently apologized to my dentist for the damage I inflicted on my molars as I ground them.

I know it's classic for mothers to be jealous of their sons' significant others and for us to think that no one is ever good enough for our boys. Was that my problem? Or was I being an intellectual snob? Just because Cyndee seems more proficient at applying lip gloss than applying logic does not mean she's a bad person. And the fact that she adores Tyler and can't keep her grasping claws off him actually shows she actually has good taste, right? But I might like her better if I could find a way to put her on mute.

"So, honey, have you talked to Jenna about her engagement?"

"She called right after she talked to you. She was pretty excited." Tyler grinned a proud big brotherly grin. He and Jenna had always been close, and I figured that Tyler had seen this engagement coming long before the rest of us.

"Well, I am certainly excited!" trilled Cyndee. "Weddings are the most important day in a girl's life!" Oh really? Not being born or giving birth? Not graduating from college or starting a career you love? I clamped my big mouth firmly shut before I found myself being as rude as I yearned to be. "And it's absolutely critical to get every wedding detail just right," she continued with conviction. "Otherwise, you'll regret it for the rest of your life."

"Actually, I think the main detail to get right is the choice of a groom, wouldn't you say?" I said through clenched teeth, moving seriously toward lockjaw. Cyndee looked at me blankly; this particular detail was apparently not on her list of wedding essentials.

"Well, I think Jenna has made a good choice, Mom. I like Ryan."

"Me, too!" Cyndee enthused. "And being a veterinarian, he could provide free medical care for the entire family." Choosing to believe that Cyndee was not clever enough to mean this as an insult, I ignored her last comment.

"I like him, too, Tyler, and I think they'll be happy together. Actually, the only thing I'm concerned about is how to pay for the wedding."

"Have you talked to Dad?"

"Uh, not lately. We don't really talk all that often."

Since our divorce, Bob and I tried to be civil to one another, which we both found much easier to do if he stayed on his side of town, and I stayed on mine. Though I was much happier now than I'd been in the final years of our marriage, I still resented the way it all happened. Bob had lied to me, betrayed me, and, somewhere within the lying and betraying, found time to fritter away all of our savings and put me up to my ears in debt.

But beyond that, there was a smaller niggling hurt I'd not yet reconciled: He cheated on me with a cow. I don't mean literally a cow, but Clarisse is . . . how can I put this politely? Fat as a pregnant rhinoceros and ugly as a poorly groomed orangutan. She'll never win Miss Congeniality nor be accused of being particularly intelligent. So what has she got that I don't have? Is it her money? Her famous Double Chocolate Cream Cheese Brownies?

I can't quite believe that money and/or brownies were the only attractions. It must have been something that she did that I didn't do, or that she didn't do that I did. And now, twelve months after the divorce had been officially decreed, not knowing "why" still bothered me like a fly buzzing in the lampshade of my brain.

"Would you like me to talk to him about the wedding expenses, Mom?"

"Would you, Tyler? I know it's cowardly of me, but I just

don't know how he'll respond." Actually, as the benefactor in their little union, Clarisse was the one I was worried about. Tyler looked pensive.

"He'll probably need to clear it with Clarisse," he mused. My kid is very sharp.

"Oh, I'm sure she'd want to contribute," Cyndee declared with certainty. "Clarisse would love to be part of the family. And what better way to earn everyone's affection than by opening those money bags of hers." I can't say that I appreciated Cyndee's assessment of human nature, but I hoped her conclusion was correct.

Finally, Cyndee headed off to the "little girls' room" (personally, I hadn't gone to the "little girls' room" since I was a little girl) to powder her perfectly powdered nose. Admit it, Cyndee! You're going to pee! Ack! I really had to get a grip on myself before I said some of those deliciously rude thoughts out loud. At least I had a few precious moments alone with Tyler.

"Mom, I wanted to tell you about something while Cyndee is gone."

"What is it, honey?" Ah-ha! Maybe he was ready to break up with her! Maybe he wants advice on how to let her down gently! Maybe he needs help arranging for her to be kidnapped and sent to Bulgaria! My mind raced through several delightful scenarios before it crashed into Tyler's next words:

"Well, Cyndee wants to have my baby."

I spewed out a mouthful of green tea, then recovered nicely by going into a coughing fit. Deep breath. So if I had a pair of kings, a four . . .

"Oh really?" I said in as neutral a tone as I could produce, considering I was working on a heart attack at that particular moment.

"Yes, Mom, she just started talking about it the other day. She said she got the idea remembering Lady Bird Johnson's campaign to beautify America. She thinks that we both have excellent genes, and it would be a contribution to society."

I waited for the little ducky to come down from the ceiling and the laugh track to start. Nothing. Obviously Tyler was besotted beyond reason; in his normal state, he would have doubled over in laughter after a line like that. Tyler was waiting patiently for a response. I think it was too late (by several years) for *"That's it! You're grounded, young man!"*

"So, um, does this mean you two will get married?"

"I don't know. That wasn't part of the discussion."

"Oh. But do you love her?"

"It's really too early to say for sure, Mom. This isn't really about the two of us."

Ah, I see. It's too early to tell if he loves her but not too early to discuss having a child. In the good old days we had two simple scenarios: either a) some wayward wastrel of a man knocks up the innocent maiden or b) the conniving seductress leads a naïve young man astray so she can force him to marry her. I don't recall that we had a scenario c: two intelligent young people (okay, one intelligent young person and one with the brain of a curling iron) plan to create offspring to enhance the gene pool. This one had me totally stumped. I pulled out the line I always use when I'm feeling clueless as a parent.

"So honey, what do you think about all this?"

"I don't know yet, Mom. There's a lot to consider, and I haven't really had time to think it through. Don't let Cyndee know that you and I talked about it. I just wanted to tell someone, and I know I can tell you anything, Mom. You're such a good listener. You're always objective, and you're not the kind of mom who likes to interfere or poke your nose in my business. You always let me figure things out myself. I appreciate that."

No! I AM the kind of mother who likes to interfere! I'm really very good at it! Watch me! I'll poke my nose in so far that George W will look like an isolationist in comparison! Run, Tyler, run! Run away and hide out in Canada, grow a beard, and acquire an accent! But don't, under any circumstances, make a baby with that woman!

Cyndee with an ee returned to the table. "Everybody happy?" she chirped. I wondered if the remains of my fortune cookie were sharp enough to slit her throat.

Parenting is like riding a roller coaster: Strap yourself in, don't look down, scream like crazy, and know that sometimes you have to go no-handsies. And if you are really smart, you wait to throw up until the ride is over. I had lucked out; my kids have given me relatively little trouble, but no parent can remain totally unbruised through the ride.

Was this particular issue covered in any of my parenting manuals? I had read every book Dr. Spock had ever written (and a few by Mr. Spock that were pretty good, too). But I don't recall one titled *Will Your Son Become a Sperm*

Donor? A Mother's Practical Guide to Protecting Her Son from Conniving Hussies.

Back home later that night, I discussed the whole situation with Spud and Alli. If you're not the kind of person who discusses problems with your pets, well, as they say, "sucks to be you." I don't know about cats or gerbils, but dogs are terrific listeners. They are invariably sympathetic. They never butt in with ill-conceived opinions or impractical suggestions. No matter what you confess to them, they still think you're brilliant and terrific. And they are much less expensive than a therapist; you can buy a lot of doggy cookies for 150 bucks an hour.

"So this bitch (as I was telling the story to my dogs, bitch was merely descriptive, not pejorative) wants to, uh, mate with your boy. Her conformation isn't bad, but her temperament seems a bit unstable, and she's very yappy if you ask me."

Spud barked a question.

"Uh, yes, I think she's always in heat, Spud."

Alli put her paw on my thigh and looked meaningfully in my eyes.

"No, Alli, I don't think I could have Tyler fixed."

The two beagles stretched out at my feet in deep contemplation of the problem. Alli's contemplation was so deep that within minutes she was snoring.

"I don't know what they would do with the litter. I certainly want to be a grandma. I would make a terrific grandma, don't you think, Spud?" His eyes were shut, but he thumped his tail in obvious agreement. "Of course, I don't knit, so I couldn't make those little baby blankets, and I get nauseous just thinking about riding carousels . . ." My mind spun off in all the ways I would and wouldn't make a terrific grandma.

I intend to be an Auntie Mame kind of grandmother. I'll take the little ones on adventures I had never, being a very responsible parent, allowed my kids to experience. Like paint ball or bungee jumping! I won't worry about making sure the grandkids have three square meals a day; that's a parent's job. As grandparent, I can feed them all the foods the American Dental Association warns against, and I can even introduce them to new foods. Like sushi! I'll let them get muddy and have food fights; we'll stay up way past their bedtime, and I'll let them sleep in their clothes if they feel like it. I will be an awesome grandma!

"But I don't want to become a grandma this way, some kind of genetic experiment. Didn't George Orwell write about something like this? Or was it George Carlin? What if smart genes aren't dominant and the kid ends up with Cyndee's stupid genes? Can you just imagine a houseful of little Cyndees?" Spud moaned sympathetically.

What could have possibly gotten into Tyler? For his entire life, he had been levelheaded and directed and mature for his age and . . . actually, maybe that was the problem. Maybe Tyler had spent too much of his childhood being adult. Maybe he was revisiting the crazy adolescence he avoided the first time through. Maybe his hormones had finally gotten the best of him after so many years of suppressing them to reach his goals. Maybe Cyndee represented all the wild flings he had never permitted himself to have before. Or maybe Cyndee had hypnotized him or fed him some kind of mind-altering drug. Maybe Cyndee was really a devious alien from a cruel and desperate planet that needed the sperm of young attorneys to keep its civilization alive . . . And maybe I needed to get some sleep before my imagination led me to desperate measures involving weapons more lethal than fortune cookies.

I crawled into bed, somehow knowing that I wouldn't be much more successful in getting to sleep than I'd been the previous two nights. What happened to my relaxing, tennies-breaking-in weekend? I'd been home less than forty-eight hours, and my personal universe had spun completely out of control. My best friends were certifiable, my daughter was getting married and I had no way to pay for it, my sometimes-date was afraid I might have honorable intentions, and my son was the potential sperm donor for a lamebrain vixen with enhanced mammary glands. I always hesitate to say this, but was there anything else that could possibly go wrong?

Is that the theme music from *Jaws* I hear?

To Do Tomorrow:
Break in Tennies
Buy Zero Population Growth *for Tyler*
Find way to pay for wedding (bake sale? garage sale?
    14 years' salary advance?)
Find ~~new friends~~ *three-for-one psychotherapy special*
  (G, M, J)

Chapter 8

During the two weeks after the weekend when *everything* seemed to go wrong, nothing new went wrong. But then again, the things that had previously gone wrong did not substantially improve. I knew this because my To-Do lists read like e. e. cummings and my phone rang constantly for fourteen days.

Brrng!

". . . I just stare at the case files on my desk and can't figure out where to begin. I walk into a room and I can't remember why I'm there. And today I couldn't even remember the combination to my gym locker. I am becoming so stupid that I can hardly function! Angie, what am I going to do?"

"But, Gwen, even Einstein didn't bother remembering little things like locker combinations."

"He didn't?"

"No, he didn't. I read his biography a while back. He used to say that he never cluttered his brain with items that are easy to reference."

"Really?"

"Yes. Of course, he was working on the Theory of Relativity at the time, which I suppose took up a lot of brain space. So perhaps there wasn't any room left for the small stuff." There was a long pause. "You're not working on some groundbreaking scientific hypothesis, are you Gwen?"

"No." Anther pause. "Angie?"

"Yes?"

"Was that story supposed to make me feel better?"

"Uh, yes."

"It didn't."

"Oh."

Brrng!

"I'm beginning to wish that I'd been born a man."

"You do? What on earth makes you say that, Marie?"

"Men are free to do as they wish. They can make obscene gestures to idiots in traffic, yell rude things to incompetent referees, pick their noses, and scratch their crotches—all without ruining their reputations."

"Oh, well, gosh, Marie, I see your point. Those are all things I've always yearned to do."

"Oh, Angie, it's not the specifics! It's that men are free to express themselves, especially their anger. Women just don't have a way to do that."

"Express anger? That's not true. There are some very famous women who were pretty darn good at expressing their anger. Lizzie Borden comes to mind, or What's Her Name Bobbitt." There was a heavy silence. "Uh, Marie, not that I want to give you any ideas . . ."

Brrng!

"Angie, the point you're missing about younger men is that they are relatively coot-proof."

"I'm afraid to ask this, Jess, but what exactly is 'coot-proof'?"

"You know, old coots. Those guys at four-way stop signs who wave everybody through as if they'd been ordained as ground traffic controllers."

"The old guys who do that hack, hack, hack, and spit thing? Who wear their trousers at armpit level?"

"Exactly. It's a proven fact that 87 percent of all men become old coots as they age."

"What about the other 13 percent?"

"They must die young."

"Oh."

"So if we hook up with men our own age, they'll become old coots within just a few years. But younger men still have several cootless years in them . . ."

Brrng!

"Mom, I talked to Ryan's mom over the phone. She says they have about seventy-five people to add to the guest list. That brings us to three hundred and twenty-five guests. Is that too many for a sit-down dinner?"

Brrng!

"Mom, exactly how much does it cost to raise a child? Cyndee says we should assume that she/he will be brilliant and get scholarships. And what do you think about the names Tylee if it's a girl or Cynder if it's a boy? Cyndee thought combining our two names would . . ."

Brrng!

"Um, Angie, I've been called out of town again, and I'm not sure when I'll be back. I'm afraid I have to cancel our date Friday. Would next Thursday work . . . ?"

Brrng!

"Mrs. Hawkins, we at Dental Deluxe are just calling to let you know that you might be paying too much for your periodontal work and we have a special sale for periodontal services happening right now that could save you hundreds of dollars."

"Uh, but I don't need to have any periodontal work done."

"I see. Any problems with cracked windshields? We happen to be in a joint venture with Cracks 'R Us and . . ."

By the end of those two weeks, my left eye went into spasm every time the phone rang, and I had become particularly adroit with caller ID. I finally stopped answering my phone entirely. I knew it was my duty to *be there* for everyone, but couldn't I *be there* for everyone from someplace else? Some distant, phoneless place else? Maybe Pago Pago?

Of course, I couldn't spend all of my time answering the phone and *being there* for the people in my life. I also had to work. I'm an asset manager, and the assets that I manage are retail centers and office buildings. Being an asset manager means that I am a Big Picture Guy (you know, someone who doesn't actually *do* anything, but who manages people who supervise people who do actual work). This was fortunate because my lack of sleep and the persistent distraction of my family and friends made me particularly ineffective on the job. But being a Big Picture Guy, who would know the difference? The key to being a good

Big Picture Guy is to throw every decision back on someone who actually knows something about it. Take for instance, the critical issue of janitorial contracts:

"Angie, if we give SactoClean the janitorial contract for that building, they will charge thirty-seven cents per roll of toilet paper whereas Janico would charge only thirty-three cents." Donna, my property manager, is very good at her job because she finds this mind-numbing minutia fascinating. As the Big Picture Guy, I ask the Big Picture Question:

"So Donna, how many rolls annually do you think they will, um, consume at that site?"

"By my calculations, based on the ratio of men to women in that building and availability of soda machines on each floor . . ."

See? Even the forty-third president of the United States could have handled my job.

It is during this time that I officially entered the realm of sleep deprivation. After forty-nine years of Olympic-quality sleeping, I now struggled to get even forty winks (a phrase which has never made much sense to me: How much winking can you do while asleep?). I tried all sorts of things: taking calcium magnesium at night, reading the dictionary (it got so darned interesting right after angkat that I couldn't put it down), taking a warm bath (I fell asleep in the tub, wrinkled up like a raisin, and after I toweled off, I was even more awake than I'd been before. But I was very, very clean.). I even tried drinking warm milk (which turns out to be as disgusting as I'd feared). I ate turkey before retiring, opened all the windows for better ventilation, played soft music—none of it got me any closer to sleep.

My circadian rhythms were beating to a different drummer I guess. A very uncoordinated drummer.

I looked up sleep deprivation on the Internet and found all of my symptoms: tiredness (well, duh!), irritability, and loss of the ability to act and think coherently. Subjects in extended sleep-deprivation experiments even reported hallucinations. According to a Stanford study, insomnia like mine creates a huge "sleep debt" that could only be re-paid one way: by sleeping all of the sleep I'd not slept over the prior two weeks. Given my condition, I calculated that I'd have to sleep straight through Labor Day.

I was exhausted every day; it was only a question of ex-actly how exhausted. To keep tabs on myself, I developed my own sleep-deprivation grading system to score my symptoms:

Grade One: burning eyes; incessant yawning; general stumbling, bumbling, and mumbling incidents

Grade Two: the above symptoms, plus inability to keep eyes open during extended conference calls

Grade Three: all symptoms above, plus the urge to strangle other participants on extended conference calls

Grade Four: inability to complete complex mental tasks; loss of certain vocabulary words, plus all of the, uh, whatchamajigs above

Grade Five: all symptoms above, plus inability to keep track of time, date, physical location, or one's own name

Grade Six: inability to complete thoughts or . . .

Grade Seven: all symptoms above, plus bizarre thoughts and fantasies leading to paranoia, euphoria, or hypothermia

Grade Eight: interactive, holographic quality halluci-nations

If my symptoms went beyond Grade Eight, I'm sure I'd be lying in a pine box with lilies on my chest. Actually, that didn't sound too bad . . .

At the end of that second week of sleepless nights and unproductive days, I invited my three best friends to join me for a glass of wine and hors d'ouevres. It would be efficient, allowing me to *be there* for all three of them at once. Plus (per a theory I developed during a Grade Four sleep-deprived moment), bringing them together might neutralize their wackiness. Like two negatives make a positive or two neutrons and an ion make . . . okay so perhaps my scientific rationale was weak. But maybe we could just eat and drink ourselves into oblivion together.

The four of us settled on my tiny porch and watched Spud and Alli perform their evening sentry duties, securing the perimeter of the yard. Thus far, we had been protected from a sinister grandma with a baby stroller, a menacing pair of Brownies selling Girl Scout cookies, and three squirrels of dubious character. I felt safe.

Actually, until just recently you wouldn't have found my three friends in the same space together even with the bribe of free wine and food. For most of my adult life, these three friends had pointedly and determinedly avoided each other. I wish I could say that they had just matured out of their mutual antipathy and mellowed with age. But the truth is that I got myself into such a pickle a few months back that it took all three of them working together to pull me out. That project apparently created a deep bond between them, a can-you-believe-Angie-is-so-clueless? kind of bond that proved to be stronger than my boiled icing. So it was a new pleasure to have them all together.

"Damn, life's a bitch, isn't it?" Marie growled. Okay, so maybe not a pleasure to have them together. Maybe relaxing is a better word . . .

"Oooo! But I think life is thrilling!" Jessica's shrill voice hit octaves that made Spud moan. She shuddered and shivered, rubbing her arms frantically. "Oooo! The energy is so strong tonight!" Okay, so maybe the gathering was not relaxing. But interesting . . .

"Huh? Oh, right, I suppose so. What were you saying? God, I'm tired. Anybody have the time? I seem to have misplaced my watch. Again." Gwen slouched in her chair, the antithesis of her usually elegant and dynamic posture, and continued mumbling incoherently into her wineglass. Okay, so not very interesting . . .

Actually, this gathering featured four of the Seven Dwarfs. I, of course, was Sleepy and my guests filled in as Dopey, Grumpy, and Horny (the X-rated dwarf Disney has concealed all these years). Quite a party. I can't say that we really had conversation that evening. More like several soliloquies that periodically bumped into one another.

"I was furious! I sat in the drive-through, waiting and waiting, until this surly, mumbly kid asked for my order. Then, of course, he didn't listen to a word I said. I had to repeat my order four times. Four times! I was so mad when I got to the drive-up window I could have pulled his scrawny little neck through the . . ." Marie hammered each of her frustrations home by slamming her glass against the deck chair. Fortunately, we were using my special-occasion wineglasses, the ones made of tractor-trailer-quality plastic.

"Speaking of driving, I lost my car at the airport last week. At least I think it was last week. Maybe the week before. Anyway, I had to call the parking lot attendant. He came in a truck to drive me around. We drove around and around and around because I couldn't remember my license plate number. Or which car I had brought to the airport. Or if I'd even brought a car to the airport . . ." Gwen's voice trailed off as she stared into her wine, perhaps expecting her car to appear there.

"What a Cosmic Coincidence! I was at the airport last week, too! I had just met a gorgeous boy, uh, man, and on the spur of the moment, we decided to fly to Vegas for the weekend! I reserved a beautiful room for us at the Bellagio, though I have to confess," Jess disclosed coyly, "we didn't waste much time sleeping in it . . ."

"I haven't gotten much sleep lately either. I stay up most of the night thinking and worrying, especially about Tyler. I can't understand why he is so enamored of that Cyndee person. And to even consider having her child! It's just not like him to let sex take over his brain . . ."

"Men are all like that, Angie," Marie proclaimed angrily. "Take Jack. Crawling all over me until a couple of weeks ago. Then poof! Nothing. He's avoiding me like the plague. Says I'm not acting like myself. He seems almost afraid of me."

"Well, I am definitely not acting like myself lately," Gwen, who never whines, whined. "More like Goldie Hawn or Gracie Allen. Did you know Gracie Allen was exceptionally intelligent underneath? Apparently, it drove her to the brink of insanity to have to act so dingy all the time. I know exactly how she feels . . ."

"Well, sometimes I feel like I'm going insane, thinking about sex all the time. Fortunately for me," Jess added, smiling lasciviously, "there are plenty of men out there who are happy to accommodate 'the urge,' if you know what I mean . . ."

"Well, you're certainly doing better than I am," I groused. "I've got two guys on my romantic options list who still haven't even asked me out. And then there's Tim. I really like Tim, but he's out of town all the time. Then he calls up at the last minute and seems irked that I can't drop everything and get together with him. It's so irritating! Of course, I've been pretty busy myself, so . . ."

"You know what's really irritating, that little pat-pat thing!" Marie said heatedly. "I hate it when a man does that! That patronizing little pat-pat on the head, like you're a pet poodle or something! It's so condescending! Jack did that to me last night, and I nearly ripped his head off. Do you think I overreacted?"

We took a moment to contemplate the pat-pat thing and being patronized in general. Most of us agreed that the pat-pat thing was worthy of ripping off someone's head. Most of us, that is, except for Spud who, we all graciously granted, really did have more experience with pat-pats than the rest of us. Spud argued, via poignant looks and tail gestures, that the pat-pat thing was really a sign of affection and should not be taken as offensive. Alli remained silent on the issue, her loyalties divided. We agreed to disagree, patted Spud on the head, and poured some more wine.

"Talk about patronizing! How about being patronized by your own secretary? Mine keeps arranging and rearranging the stacks in my office, even putting bright little sticky notes on them. As if I didn't know what I'm supposed to do next! Which, well, actually, I don't," Gwen confessed sadly. "I used to whip through those stacks and clear off my desk every day. Now I can't get through any of it. I've got stacks on the floor, on the guest chair, on top of the file cabinet—everywhere! It's making me nuts!"

"Well, I'll tell you what's making me nuts: this itchy, twitchy thing. Nothing helps! It feels like a thousand ants crawling all over me, my scalp, my legs . . ." Jess's narrative got to all of us, and the conversation (or colliding monologues) died for a few moments amidst general scratching, slapping, and fidgeting.

"Is it particularly warm this evening?" Marie asked, looking slightly flushed.

"Hmmm. I'm pretty warm myself." Gwen fanned herself with her cocktail napkin.

"Very warm," Jess agreed, placing her cool glass of Chardonnay against her forehead.

My thermostat must have been malfunctioning. The cool delta breezes were blowing, and I shivered in my sweater. Maybe there was something wrong with me. Maybe body temperatures or metabolisms change if you don't get enough sleep. A Grade Six symptom perhaps. The four of us sat in silence for a few more moments, each of us contemplating separate miseries.

"Well, if nothing else, the one positive note in my life is that Jenna is getting married," I said brightly. "Even though I'm not sure yet how I'll pay for it," I remembered glumly.

"Oh, that's right! Can you imagine? Our little Jenna getting married!" Marie's voice and face softened as they hadn't for weeks.

"She'll be such a beautiful bride, Angie! I really should compare her astrological chart with Ryan's to see how their houses line up," Jess offered, finally thinking of something beyond her overly charged root chakra.

Even Gwen came alive at the thought of Jenna's wedding. "Why don't we throw a party for her? A wedding dress party! As her official bridesmaids, I think it's our duty! I have a former client who owns an exquisite, high-end bridal shop. We could do it there."

"Oh, Gwen, I don't even know what kind of budget we have. I don't think high-end will be . . ."

"Oh, don't worry about it, Angie. She'll do it for me as a favor. We can figure out what kind of dress Jenna wants, and you can have it made elsewhere."

"And I could get someone to cater it. David Berkeley owes me a lot of favors for jobs I've gotten him . . ." Marie's face glowed in anticipation.

"Oh, and I think I can score us some great wine for the party! There's this cutest guy at the winery at Lake Almanor. I'm sure I could persuade him to . . ."

What is it with us women? We might appear totally self-absorbed in our own personal issues, but most of us are easily diverted when someone else's happiness is at stake. We don't strut around on life's stage as the divas of every production, but gladly perform as the Greek chorus for those we cherish—supporting them, cheering them on, giving them shoulders to cry on.

Our excitement for Jenna and her upcoming wedding broke through our recent self-inflicted insanities and seemed to snap all four of us back to ourselves. We twittered and giggled for the rest of the evening, drawing up our plan of action to organize Jenna's wedding dress party.

Team To-Do List:
  Gwen: Arrange for bridal salon
  Marie: Contact David Berkeley's for food
  Jess: Do <u>whatever necessary</u> to get wine
  Angie: Get some sleep

Chapter 9

They may be difficult, and they may be slightly crazy, but to a woman my best friends are awesome party planners. Gwen twisted the arm of her bridal shop client to reserve the salon for the entire afternoon for us alone. Marie convinced David Berkeley's to bring its A-list of hors d'oeuvres, and I didn't even want to ask what Jess did to score that case of superb wine for us. Jenna had chosen her bridesmaids well. As for me? All I did was show up. (Jenna chose her bridesmaids well, but her mother was chosen for her.)

The salon was very chic with fresh flowers, stunning artwork, and obviously expensive furnishings. The owner, Grace, welcomed us at the door and led us to a private salon in the back. Grace wore an elegant but simple black dress adorned with a hand-painted silk scarf draped gracefully over one shoulder, held in place by an exquisite brooch. Her staff, who hovered nearby, were similarly attired. This was not Brides 'R Us.

"I won a settlement for Grace in a sexual harassment suit. It paid for the entire salon," Gwen whispered in my ear. "She owes me big-time."

"My gosh," Jessica inserted. "She must have been really harassed." Jess sounded slightly envious, but I couldn't tell if she was envious of the settlement or the harassing itself.

"Let me introduce Mona," Grace said graciously. "Mona will be Jenna's fitter."

"Mom!" Jenna whispered excitedly. "I have my own fitter!"

Jenna was having the time of her life. In truth, maybe our weddings are the only times we get to live out those fairy tales we grow up on. We start life humming "Someday My Prince Will Come" then all too quickly learn the words to "Working Nine to Five." Where are the princes? Where are the balls? Where are the glass slippers? Not that I think any of us want our whole lives to be sugar-spun and moon-glowed, but a little magic dust every now and then would be good for our feminine souls, don't you think?

Jenna and her fitter headed behind the stage area to get her into the first dress. The four of us settled into the luxurious sofas and poured the wine. Everything was lovely! The stage was set, the wine was poured, the food was on, and disaster struck.

Disaster struck in the form of the not-so-lovely, not-so-welcome Clarisse, followed closely by the "oh my gosh, did I really marry him?" Bob.

"Hello, ladies. I'm so happy to see you could be here while we pick out Jenna's dress. Ah! Hors d'oeuvres!" Clarisse turned her considerable bulk toward the food table as Bob positioned himself awkwardly in a chair at the far corner of the room.

"Angie!" Jessica's sharp elbow fractured my ribs. "Did you invite her?"

"Of course she didn't!" Gwen hissed. "Snap to, Angie. You look like you left your brain at the bus stop."

"Well, however they got here, Clarisse is plowing through our hors d'ouevres like a swarm of locusts. Is Bob here to represent the frogs or the boils?" Marie scowled.

"So what do you think of this one? I think it's kind of cute." Jenna bounced out of the fitting room onto the stage, then screeched to an awkward halt as she took in the presence of her dad and Clarisse. "Oh, hi. Um, I'm glad you could be here." Jenna looked at me with an apologetic shrug.

"I don't like it. The waistline is too high, and I hate the sleeves. Go to the next one." Clarisse sipped her glass of wine and waved a dismissal; the Evil Stepmother had spoken. This was clearly not going to be the festive party we had envisioned.

"Why that fat . . . !" Marie started up from beside me, but I yanked her back down.

"Who crowned her fashion queen?" Jessica muttered.

"Relax, everybody. She's just trying to become part of the family," I whispered. I couldn't believe I was repeating nonsense I'd heard from Cyndee.

Jenna came out in the next dress with a little less bounce. "So what does everyone think of this one?"

"Oh, Jenna, it's adorable and I love those . . ." Gwen started.

"Too revealing for your age, Jenna. It won't do at all. You're not supposed to look sexy at your wedding. You're supposed to look pure. Try again." Clarisse turned decisively back to her plate of food as Jenna turned self-consciously back to the dressing room. I could feel the steam rising out of Gwen . . . or was it Jess? . . . or was it Marie? All three were getting pretty hot.

As for me, I was completely stupefied, stunned stupid, shocked speechless. I looked to Bob for help, but he wouldn't meet my eye (are we surprised?). I knew Clarisse might be paying for a substantial part of the wedding, so perhaps it was only fair that she have a say in choosing the dress. I didn't want to overreact and wreck Jenna's party. So I vowed to keep myself (and my steaming friends) calm, cool, collected. We were adults. We could maintain decorum in an adultlike manner. I sat up straighter and thought of aces and sevens with jacks and queens. Jenna came out once more, slowly this time, enthusiasm definitely dampened.

"So do you think . . . ?" she started hesitantly.

"Oh, God! That's the worst one yet," Clarisse announced. "You look like Glinda the Good Witch of the North." Jenna's lower lip started to tremble.

"And you certainly would know, Clarisse," I roared as I stood, "being the Wicked Witch of the West!" Everyone gasped, even me. So much for calm, cool, collected.

"How dare you come in here and throw your weight around!" I stomped over to stand directly in front of Clarisse. "This is *my* daughter and *her* wedding, and you will get your huge fricking nose and other body parts out of it!" Clarisse rose from the sofa, all 234 pounds of her in charging-rhino mode. We would have stood nose to nose if not for the large gap created by her 48DDD bosom.

"Angie, if you want to see one penny from me for this wedding, you will sit down and be quiet right now," she said menacingly.

This was a woman who, if she chose to sit on me, could flatten me to the thinness of matzos. But my maternal adrenaline was pumping, and I knew no fear. My beautiful baby girl was going to have the wedding dress of her dreams even if it cost me my sorry little existence on this planet! "And, Clarisse, if you want to leave this salon alive and with all your body parts intact, you will sit down and shut up and pretend you don't exist." My mouth had taken on a power of its own.

We stood facing one another, Queen Kong meets Thumbelina, and I was pretty sure that this would be my final moment, swatted like a fly into oblivion by one of Clarisse's humongous arms. How would the obituary read? *She died in defense of her daughter's right to choose her sleeve style.* Just as my life started flashing before me (I was still at the part where Robbie Schumacher and I were making out behind the junior high school gym), I felt a presence behind me, my three best friends rising to my support. Combining all four of us, we might even qualify for Clarisse's weight class.

Clarisse's look of defiance wavered as she faced the troops behind me. "Don't," I said, with Mafioso certainty, "mess with me."

It's apparently fortunate that I could not actually see the cavalry at my back: Marie was armed with a fistful of bread sticks, Gwen brandished a rolled-up brides' magazine, and Jessica held a silk tulip menacingly above her head. Fairy godmothers turned Green Berets, their fury was unmistakable, but their chosen weapons weren't likely to be banned by the Antiproliferation Treaty anytime soon.

Clarisse tried one last stand. "Angie, either I get to plan this wedding, or you'll not get any financial support from me. Then what will you do?"

"We don't need your money, and we wouldn't stoop to take one cent from you, Clarisse," I said with a certainty that only the insanity of raw nerves could produce. "This is my daughter's wedding, and she will plan it as she sees fit! You can leave now."

Clarisse paused for a moment before turning her massive rump to head out the door. Bob, with an uncomfortable shrug and a small wave to Jenna, followed closely behind.

None of us moved for a few moments after the two of them left the salon. I think we were all evaluating just how crazy the last few minutes had been and how much of that craziness we each had contributed. The silence was broken by the sound of someone clapping. Someone else took it up and I looked around to see Grace and her entire staff applauding enthusiastically.

"Oh," Grace breathed, "I can't tell you how many times we've wanted to do that, Mrs. Hawkins!"

"The women who come in here, pushing their poor young daughters around, stomping all over a young girl's dream, I could kill them! It's awful to watch!" added Mona, with heartfelt passion.

"Mom, you were great!" Jenna threw her arms around

me in a strangling hug. "And don't worry; we'll be careful with expenses."

"Well, that certainly was invigorating." Gwen smiled, almost like her old feisty self. "Though you nearly got us all killed, Angie."

"That was like the scene in *Jurassic Park*. Not the one in the port-a-potty—God, I was constipated for weeks after that one!—but the one where the huge dinosaur stomps up to the little kids . . ." Jess breathed, twitching and itching excitedly.

"One swish of that huge tail of hers, and we would have been toast. Hey! *Tyrannosaurus rex* ate all our food!" Marie groused.

"Not to worry; I'll order more. This has been a wonderful event, and we can't let it end!" Grace gushed. "Mona, help Jenna into more dresses. This bride deserves to have only the best!" Mona and the rest of the staff scurried around like royal ladies-in-waiting, pampering the four of us and fawning over Princess Jenna.

And Jenna does deserve the best. But was I the only one who recognized that my "heroics" had just ruined our only chance of bankrolling the best for her? Marie poured more wine into my glass. I tried to keep my happy face in place as I gulped it down and requested a refill. And then another . . .

Perhaps I drank a little too much wine that afternoon because Jenna insisted on driving me home. She fed Spud and Alli before she left, saying something about me being snockered and not wanting them to starve while I sobered up. Hrrmph! As I wobbled around trying to figure out how to get undressed, the phone rang.

"Unh-huh."

"Angie? Is that you?" Tim's voice sounded uncertain.

"Yesh, uh, yes, it's me."

"Are you okay?"

"Unh-huh. Back from a little party." I startled myself with a hiccup. Tim started to laugh.

"Well, sounds like another wild time. What was it this time?"

Oh, heck! I couldn't tell him about it because I wasn't supposed to say the word "wedding." Never, never, ever say the word "wedding." Or the word "marriage." Or the "L" word or that word that begins with 'f . . .' "We had a little sort of, kinda like, party for Jenna."

"Like a wedding shower or something?"

Okay, so if he says the "W" word first, does that mean I can say it? I stumbled over to the bookcase to find my copy of *The Rules* to get a ruling. *The Rules* to get a ruling—ha-ha! I started to giggle.

"Uh, Angie, maybe this isn't the best time to talk."

"Why not? Are you busy? I'm not busy." I knocked over the stack of books next to my bed as I flopped back on the pillows.

Tim laughed again. He really does have a nice laugh, and a nice voice, and nice hands, and a nice ass . . .

"I have to fly to Detroit tomorrow, but I was calling to see if we could go out for dinner when I get back in town. A week from Monday?"

"Let me get my Plane Pilot."

" 'Plane' Pilot?"

"Yesh. So I have the little poker and I'm poking the little 'M' for Monday and—nope, I can't do it. It says I'm seeing Jessica that night."

"Ah-ha. So could you poke the little 'W' and see if you're free that Wednesday then?"

"Yes, I could do that. I am poking the little 'W' and it says—nope, I am having dinner with Lilah and Jenna that night. Should I poke the next letter?"

"No. Unfortunately, I leave town again for several days after that. I won't be back until the following Wednesday."

"So I am poking the little 'W' for the next week. Uh-oh, I have to go to the dentist at five o'clock. I couldn't go out to dinner with you because I talk very shlurrily after I go to the dentist."

"You're talking very 'shlurrily' right now."

"I am?"

"Yes. Okay, Angie, why don't we have lunch that day?"

"Okey dokey, artichokey!" I giggled and lay back on the bed and attempted to tap Tim's name into the calendar.

"Angie, you're not going anywhere tonight, are you?"

"Nope. Are you? Wanna come visit?"

"Tempting, but no, I'd better not. Get some sleep. Sweet dreams." At least I think that's what he said. I'm actually not positive because my snoring was too loud by then to hear his last words.

The trouble with a drunken sleep is that it's not a solid sleep. I woke up at about midnight with an awful taste in my mouth, a pounding headache, and a vague sense that I had just embarrassed myself. Was it Clarisse? I groaned, re-membering the scene at the bridal salon. But there was something else, something after . . .

This was not going to be a good night. My stomach felt awful. My head felt awful. My psyche felt awful knowing that my big mouth had cut off all sources of funds for Jenna's wedding. Well, maybe not all sources. There was still Lilah. But even Lilah might rescind her offer of assis-tance when she hears how nasty I was to "that woman." Lilah may not like Clarisse, but she absolutely detests pub-lic brawls (as opposed to public spectacles which Lilah adores, especially if she's in the middle of them). Maybe Lilah will actually feel sorry for Clarisse when she hears all the despicable things I said. Heck, when Lilah finds out about my outrageous behavior, she just may give Clarisse her name back and I'll become "that woman," the shrew her precious son never should have married in the first place.

Did I really call Clarisse "Wicked Witch of the West"? What's wrong with me? I hadn't felt such a rage since 1988 when some Fascist preschool teacher reprimanded Jenna for coloring the trees in her coloring book pink and purple. As I recall, I had been fairly forceful with my language at that time as well, encouraging the woman to take up a ca-reer in taxidermy. (After this incident, the school insisted that a neutral third party join us for all of our parent-teacher conferences. I don't think he was armed.) But though I had, on rare occasions, lost my head and control of my mouth, I thought I'd matured out of such scenes. Apparently not. And this time I might have ruined my little girl's big day—not the kind of thought that leads to peaceful sleep. I watched my clock tick through the minutes: 2:37, 2:38, 2:39 . . .

To-Do's:

~~Go visit Clarisse to apologize~~
~~Call Clarisse to apologize~~
~~E-mail Clarisse to apologize~~
Ask Jenna re: eloping (Chapel O' Love?)

Chapter 10

If I were a sitcom, I would have been canceled by then. Honestly, some expensive-suited, high-powered studio exec with a nervous eye twitch and tassels on his loafers would have taken one look at this period of my life and deep-sixed it:

"No, no, no! Too many plotlines! She can't have everything in her life go wrong at the same time. One problem per week, that's the limit! And she's the star of the show. How come this is all about everybody else?"

Well, welcome to the real world, pal. In the real world, at least in my real world, sticky situations don't line up politely to be neatly resolved in half hour segments. They stumble over each other in a chaotic heap, clamoring for attention. And sometimes the star of the show has her hands full just keeping the cast from diving into the orchestra pit. My friends went back to acting like escapees from an asylum, and my own bout of temporary insanity threatened to ruin the one happy plotline of the show,

Jenna's wedding. I hadn't heard much from Tyler; would my next notice be an invitation to Cyndee's baby shower?

I had perfected insomnia and was running on an average of four hours of sleep per night. My worry stream flowed nonstop, without even pausing for punctuation or potty breaks: Maybe I could make Jenna's dress myself though of course that would mean I have to learn how to sew and the only person I know who can sew is Jessica who might not have time to help since she is so wrapped up in finding young studs which brings up the issue of Tyler who has been chosen to stud by Cyndee who can't even spell her name but then again neither can Gwen these days . . .

Jessica had insisted I join her for dinner Monday night. Did I want to go? No. Did I agree to go? Yes. She needed me to *be there* for her.

Jess instructed me to meet her at Mitch's Bahama Mama Bar and Grille, "the hottest new place in town." I arrived in time to see her teetering up the sidewalk wearing new stilettos, the kind with the nasty-looking pointy toes designed by the Wicked Witch of the West. This, of course, reminded me of Clarisse, which reminded me of the wedding, which reminded me of Jenna, which reminded me of Tyler and . . .

"New shoes, Jess?"

"Don't you love them, Angie? I think they show off my legs nicely."

Jessica does have nice legs, and they were getting quite a workout as they struggled to keep her from toppling over. She walked like a character from *Night of the Living Dead*.

Until tonight, I don't think I'd ever seen her in anything higher than *Birkenstocks*.

"Jess, you look kind of, uh, different."

"Oh, I've just updated my makeup and my overall look." She looked like she had updated it to the Twiggy trend of the sixties with ghostly pale lips, fluorescent colors on her lids and lashes like black widow spider legs. (What the heck is the matter with the cosmetic/fashion industry? Don't they know that some beauty trends die out because they were awful the first time through? Can't they design new ugly trends? Must we recycle the old ugly trends?) "Bet you couldn't tell that I'm wearing false eyelashes." She giggled. No, not until I got within thirty yards of her. "And look at my new nails." She held out long bloodred claws that would have made Cruella De Vil proud. Her hair, usually soft and curly, poked straight up and out in incredible angles and she wore a skirt so mini that the bottom curve of her tiny rump was exposed even in the upright position. Hard to say what might be revealed if she bent forward. "I think you'll love this place, Angie. Very hip, very cool, very now."

We entered the restaurant and were hit immediately by the eardrum-bursting noise level. The music thumped aggressively, and the crowd shrieked to be heard over it. The lighting was so dim that we had to grab each other to avoid getting lost as we made our way to a table lit by a lava lamp in a dark corner.

"Jess, this isn't your usual kind of place."

"Eh?" She cupped her hand behind her ear just like my ancient grandmother used to do. Very hip, very cool, very now.

"This isn't your usual kind of place," I shrieked.

"Thanks, yes, I'll have my usual. A glass of Chardonnay. Over there." She pointed to a throng at the end of the bar. Apparently the hottest place in town is self-serve. I picked my way carefully through the closely packed crowd, praying I'd be able to find my way back to our table.

When I had finally worked my way through the sharp elbows and toe-mashing feet of the crush at the bar, the bartender (who might or might not have been of legal drinking age) looked up expectantly.

"Two glasses of Chardonnay, please." I hollered.

"Lady, this is a martini bar."

"A what?"

"A martini bar. We serve martinis."

"Oh. Okay, two then." I waited; he waited.

"Two what?"

Was this a trick question? I think I got it right this time. "Martinis."

"What kind?"

"Uh, gin?"

"No, lady, what flavor?" He pointed to a neon-lit board that covered the entire wall behind the bar. Good grief! It displayed more flavors than Baskin-Robbins. The line behind me was getting restless, so I skimmed the vast selection quickly. Dirty Martini? Is it served in an unwashed glass? Chocolate Chip Martini? Is that with or without nuts? Cajun martini? Pork martini? Few of the choices seemed actually drinkable.

"Lady . . ."

"Okay, okay. I'll have two, uh, Apple Martinis." At least

we'd get vitamins and some roughage out of it. "No, wait. Make one of them a Mashed Banana and Chocolate Syrup Martini." That should pay Jess back for dragging me to this place.

Drinks in hand, I squirmed my way through the wall of bodies back to our table. During the trek back, I distinctly felt a hand grope my backside, but, fearing I might spill our drinks (which had cost more than my last three tanks of gas), I didn't dare turn to reprimand the perpetrator.

"What took you so long? A waitress dropped off an hors d'ouevres menu." Jess handed me a burgundy-colored menu with tiny, faint gold lettering on it. I reached into my purse to bring out my reading glasses.

"Angie, no! Put those things away! How embarrassing!"

"But I can't read it without them. Can you?"

"Sure." Jess pulled the lava lamp directly over the menu. Then, holding the menu in the tips of her fingers, she stretched out her arm to its full length until I was certain her shoulder would be dislocated. "It says, um, it says . . ." She squinted so hard her nose started to spasm. "Nope. Nothing looks good. I'm not hungry anyway."

We tried to talk. Jess has a voice that can pierce body armor, but I was getting hoarse from trying to be heard. I looked around and figured that our presence at Mitch's Bahama Mama Bar and Grille increased the average age at the establishment to twenty-four and a half. What the heck were we doing there? Someone by the bar waved at me. I smiled, not wanting to be rude.

"Jess, who is that guy? It's too dark in here, and I can't make out his face, but he keeps waving at me."

"Oh, he's probably just trying to pick you up, Angie."

"Him? He's way too young for me."

"Are you going to start that again, Angie? You've certainly become close-minded."

"Close-minded? Just because I'm not attracted to a guy who still drinks out of a sippy cup?"

"You know, you're getting extremely cynical and stodgy, Angie. It's not very attractive," Jessica huffed, smoothing her very unattractive new hairdo with her particularly unattractive false fingernails.

Oh, heck, maybe she was right. My lack of sleep was making me an old grouch; is that a Grade Four or a Grade Five symptom? I mean, really, what is wrong with dating younger men? In fact at our age, our choices were certainly slim enough already. We could date men who are older than we are, few of whom still possess original teeth, or men our own age, most of whom, if available, are as fascinating as reruns of *Mork and Mindy*. I was lucky to have my current list of options, three men who could sing along to Janis Joplin and who knew Ringo Starr before he became a miniature train conductor on a kiddie program. But maybe someday I'll run through these options and need to expand my search area to include the younger set. I just think there should be some kind of age limit, like you can't date someone younger than the oldest suit in your closet or your oldest pair of shoes. I looked around the bar. Given those criteria, no one present would make the cut. Time to do some serious closet cleaning.

Jess was engrossed in another one of her Tantric twitches. Her kudalini may have been rising with all this youthful testosterone surrounding us, but I was getting a headache.

"I'm sorry, Jess. You're undoubtedly right. So, how is it going with Chad?"

"Who?"

"Chad. The boy, uh, man I met at lunch a couple of weeks ago."

"Oh, him. I'm not seeing him anymore, Angie. You probably thought he was a little young for me." No, actually I thought he was a *lot* too young for you. My latest tube of toothpaste is older than he is.

"I've met a new man. His name is Jerrod, and he's very active and well endowed, if you know what I mean."

"I can only imagine, Jess."

"In fact, Angie, I've got a surprise for you. Jerrod is going to meet us here a little later, and I asked him to bring a friend for you."

"Please tell me that you're joking, Jess." Before I could reach across the table and wring her neck, we heard a male voice shouting across the din.

"Mom!" Both of us turned, trained as we are to respond to any call of "Mom!", and saw an attractive young man work his way through the crush. "Mom, what are you doing here?" He gave Jess a big hug and sat down.

"Sean, you remember Angie Hawkins."

"Sure." He grinned. "Last time I saw you, you made me spit out the sand I'd just eaten for breakfast. You were a lot taller then. How's Jenna?"

His youthful face did look familiar; I could still see the grit-eating toddler in his eyes and forehead. But the mud that was usually present on his little-boy chin had been replaced by a trim goatee, and he wore well-cut slacks and sport coat rather than his OshKosh B'Gosh Big Boy overalls. Sean is probably a couple of years older than Jenna, and I recalled him as an engaging, slightly rambunctious kid with a sweet temperament and a tendency to eat the inedible.

"She's getting married." I screeched over the din.

"Lucky guy. I ran into her when I was in town last year and tried to ask her out, but Jenna would have none of me. So I'm out cruising still." Sean was instantly likable. I'd have to tell Jenna that he was no longer swallowing dirt and ask if she could fix him up with one of her friends. "Actually, a friend from college is setting me up tonight. He's been dating this older woman. A real hottie from what he says. Knows all the X-rated moves. Her friend is supposed to be just as wild and willing. A little generational wisdom to be passed on tonight I think." He grinned again and winked, but his mom had turned pale.

"Uh, I've gotta go, dear. We'll talk tomorrow," Jess croaked as she bolted from the table and out toward the front door.

"Is Mom okay?"

"Uh, I think so. By the way, Sean, what is your friend's name?"

"Jerrod. Why?"

"Have a nice night, Sean. Very nice to see you again. I'll give Jenna your regards." I grabbed my purse and bolted after Jessica.

I found her in the parking lot, mumbling to herself.

"Jess? Are you okay?"

"You . . . you . . . you Jezebel!"

"Jess, what on earth are you talking about?"

"You almost had a date with my son tonight! Angie, how could you?"

"May I remind you that . . ."

"Oh, put a sock in it, Angie! That's my son, for God's sake! To even imagine that you would seduce him. It's disgusting!" And with that, she did a dramatic turn on her heel to leave. Well, that's what she *would* have done if the stupid stiletto heel had supported her dramatic turn. Instead, it snapped off and sent her crashing to the asphalt.

"Oh, my gosh, Jess! Are you okay?"

"Of course I'm not okay, you hussy! My ankle is broken. Damn, damn, damn!"

Two hours later, we had settled into the ER waiting room. Despite Jessica's protests, the staff decided that the knife victims, the elderly man suffering a heart attack, and a lady with food poisoning took priority over her tweaked ankle. I begged the nurses for some Valium to cut off Jessica's nonstop harangue about my nefarious designs on her innocent son. After forty-five minutes of listening to her tirade, the nurse in charge slipped me some tablets under the counter.

"Either she takes these, or the rest of us will have to. Or if you'd prefer to overdose her, I'll get you some more of the same and we can put her at the top of the list to get her stomach pumped." I thanked her but regretfully declined the overdose suggestion.

By the time we were ushered into the examination

room, Jessica had entered a drug-induced euphoria. She had stopped yelling at me for my "despicable deceit" and was singing show tunes, very expressively though not quite tunefully, loud enough for the entire waiting room to hear. We had heard her sing her way through *South Pacific, West Side Story,* and she had just started a spirited interpretation of *Porgy and Bess* when the attractive young doctor entered.

"So, Mrs. McIntyre, how are you feeling?"

"Oooo, much better now that you are here, Doctor." Jess batted the one eyelash that still remained attached.

"So, you fell in the parking lot of Mitch's Bahama Mama Bar and Grille. I hear that's a pretty wild place."

"Well, I do have a wild side of myself that would probably surprise you." Jessica tilted her head coquettishly and twirled her tangled hair seductively with the jagged stumps of her now broken fingernails.

The doctor flipped through Jessica's chart. "Isn't this interesting! You were born on the exact same day as my mother."

"Eiyow!" Jess howled piteously, a sound not unlike a cat landing unexpectedly in a birdbath, and flopped back on the table.

"Are you in pain again? Where does it hurt, Mrs. McIntyre?"

Jess tuned up a mournful rendition of "Nobody Knows the Trouble I've Seen" as I answered for her, "I'm pretty sure it's in the vanity region."

Chapter 11

On Wednesday night, Jenna showed up for dinner incognito. At least I think that's what she was doing, for the young woman who came to my door was totally unrecognizable as Jenna. It reminded me of the Halloween costume she put together when she was eleven. For that costume, titled "Working Mom," Jenna wore one of my business suits, painted dark circles under her eyes, carried a briefcase over one shoulder and threw a diaper over the other, then strapped two baby dolls to her legs. A big hit with the real working moms in our neighborhood, Jenna's candy haul that year was record breaking.

Only this time Jenna didn't yell, "Trick or Treat!" and there was no smile of fun and anticipation. She schlumped into the house carrying a stack of binders and wearing an outfit so bland and boring that she could have borrowed it from my closet. But the most striking part of Jenna's disguise was:

"Your hair! Jenna, what have you done to your hair?"

"Oh, this," she touched her mousey brown locks distractedly. "I just thought it was time to grow up hair-wise. So I had it dyed back to my real color."

Since none of us had seen Jenna's real color for seven years, I'm not sure how she determined that mousey brown was it. I hated it; it was just not . . . not Jenna.

Amazing, isn't it? When Jenna first dyed her hair (fluorescent green as I recall) she was fifteen. I spent that entire year feeling embarrassed and self-conscious. As I signed the waivers required by her school (*I, Angie Hawkins, acknowledge that my son/daughter has chosen to dress and/or adorn him/herself in a manner that is not conducive to a rigorous academic atmosphere and/or positive social interaction as defined by San Juan Unified School District. SJUSD Dress Code edict dated September, 15, 1965.*), I was certain that Jenna's flamboyant hair exposed my maternal inadequacy and lack of parenting skills. I prayed that she would reconsider and look "normal" again.

By the second year, I was much less self-conscious and started enjoying the reactions her hair elicited. Toddlers pointed, and screamed, "Mommy, what's wrong with that girl's hair? It's purple! Is she from outer space?" Little old ladies asked to touch it and conferred with Jenna on her technique. When she wanted to experiment with contrasting color patterns, I helped her get the zigzags ziggy and the dots round. We even discussed new hair colors as they came on the market. "Mom, do you think Bubblegum Pink would go with my skin tone?"

By the third year, I had become so accustomed to her hair that I rarely thought about it. Those lively locks were simply Jenna, a symbol of her inner uniqueness, and Jenna's hair reassured me that the world would never be colorless or boring as long as I had this daughter in my life.

Odd, isn't it? In those first two years, I would have been thrilled for her to choose the "mature" route and uncolor her hair. But now? I really missed the peacock blue. But hair is just hair, right? I had said that to myself during the fluorescent green stage; was it any less true in the mousey brown stage?

Jenna was quiet as we drove to the restaurant to meet Lilah, so I had time to deliberate on what was happening to my daughter. This deliberation, of course, quickly morphed into: Was it something I had done wrong? Had I been an inadequate mother somehow? Did I not give enough guidance? Or provide the correct foundation for a healthy blah dee blah dee, blah, blah, blah . . . We all know this song by heart, don't we? "The Bad Mommy Blues."

And if the Parental Regulatory Institute for Childrearing Knowledge and Suitability (they rarely use their acronym) comes to take away my Mommy License, would I be able to defend myself?

Point One: I have loved both my children totally and unconditionally (though this may have not been obvious in 1989 after they poured sixteen packages of Jell-O into the bathtub to see if it would get jiggly).

Point Two: I have always encouraged my kids to be themselves, not clones of *my*self (though during the years when themselves were in the Terrible Twos, I prayed that those themselves would not become the permanent themselves).

Point Three: I realize that I don't have all of the answers—and neither do they. My kids are bright and I had parented via negotiation whenever possible:

"Mom, do I have to brush my teeth every single night?"

"Absolutely not, Tyler. Of course if you don't, your teeth will rot out and you'll end up looking like Elmo—no teeth at all. And, honey, you should be aware that the Tooth Fairy won't cough up quarters for teeth that fall out due to poor dental hygiene. You decide."

"Mom, I hate school. Can't I just stay home with you today? Please?"

"Sure, sweetie, and I've got a big day planned for us. First we'll clean up the dog poop in the backyard, then knock down the cobwebs under the eaves, sweep out the garage, polish the silver . . . Jenna, where are you going?

"Gotta get dressed, Mom, or I'll miss the bus."

"Tyler, what are you doing up there on the roof? Is that your Superman cape?"

"Yep. I'm going to fly, Mom! I had a dream about it last night. I put on this cape, and I could fly, just like Superman. It was so cool!"

"Well, before you launch yourself, honey, I need to tell you that your cape isn't the flying model. We bought the walking-only version."

"We did?"

"Yes, so if you want to fly, you'll have to do it like the birds. You know what allows them to fly, don't you?"

"No. What?"

"Worms. You have to eat a lot of worms, Tyler. But I know where we can get some, so if you want to . . ."

"Uh, Mom, do you think Dad could help me get down from here?"

"Mom, can I get my eyebrow pierced?"

"No, Jenna."

"Why not?"

"Because I said so."

Okay, so granted, some of our negotiations had broken down. But I did try to get my kids to think for themselves. So dyeing her hair back to "natural" was just Jenna thinking for herself, wasn't it?

Lilah, in town for a couple of days, had to join Bob and that woman for dinner so she could only join us for a drink. She was already seated at our table when we arrived and she did a double take when she saw Jenna's hair. But Lilah, woman of the world that she is, recovered quite gracefully:

"Oh, my God! Who ruined your hair?"

"It's my natural color, Gran."

"No grandchild of mine ever had such boring hair naturally or unnaturally. What on earth were you thinking?" I gave Lilah a warning kick under the table and a stern look. "Well," she finished weakly, "I'm sure it's fashionable somewhere. Like maybe in Lithuania."

Jenna didn't seem to hear her. She brought out her stack of three ring binders, handing one to each of us.

"Okay, so it's time we all got organized over this wedding project," Jenna announced, with an air of efficiency.

"Wedding project. How romantic," Lilah murmured.

"I've been researching wedding planning on the Internet," Jenna continued. "Per recommendations, I've made up a binder for each of you with your assignments and dates by which each assignment needs to be accomplished based on an estimated wedding date of January 20. We'll set up regular status meetings to keep on track and update the binder information periodically."

"Do we get traded off the team if we don't complete our assignments per schedule?" Lilah asked. I thumped her shin firmly with my toe again.

"Gran, there's a lot of detail to cover and over two hundred tasks. I've divided them up equitably between us. But we're already late on tasks 1.1 through 1.23. We have some catching up to do as you will see if you turn to tab number two." Lilah and I numbly opened our binders to tab number two to find a Gantt chart complete with timelines and critical milestones.

"Sweet Pea, are we planning a wedding or a hostile corporate takeover?" I tried to kick Lilah again, but she scooted her leg just out of reach. I had to settle for a threatening scowl.

"Under tab three, you'll find some time-saving ideas that might help us get back on schedule."

"Oh, my! Look at this one, Angie: 'To save time the bride can prewrite her thank-you notes, leaving the giver's name and the gift item blank, to be filled in later.' Why not just send a mass e-mail, Sweet Pea, addressed To Whom It May

Concern?" Lilah wasn't quite quick enough to avoid my warning kick this time.

"I'll think about it, Gran," Jenna said, quite seriously. "Now if you will turn to tab five, I have the preliminary guest list with contact information and pertinent data. I wasn't sure if Uncle Bernie should be a five or a six. What do you two think?"

"A five or six what, Sweet Pea?"

"You know, Gran, ranking in terms of his importance. A 'one' person is absolutely most important and a 'ten' is least. Wedding planners recommend you rank everybody in case you have to cut back the guest list and to help with seating arrangements."

"Ranking your friends and relatives? That's the most ridiculous thing you've said so far!" Lilah sputtered indignantly. "Do we rank them based on table manners? Or how big a gift they might give? Are you planning to quantify exactly how much you love each person or they, you?" Jenna started to tear up at her grandmother's sharp words, and I gave Lilah another well-placed kick under the table. She scowled and gave me a harder kick back. We thrashed at each other under the table like unruly toddlers.

"Gran, I'm just trying to get organized . . ."

"Sure you are, sweetie. Look, why don't you and Gran and I just talk in general for a bit. Kind of ease into the planning. Let's all relax and have a glass of wine." Or two or three. Give us time to locate my real daughter within the stranger who sat before us.

And time to get Lilah mellowed out before she said something really nasty. Lilah was not known for her diplomacy, but she and Jenna adored each other. Lilah had been her granddaughter's chief advocate and champion since Jenna was born, defending her ferociously from the "narrowed-minded, squinty-eyed, chinless, gutless fascists" who dared criticize her (a group that had, more than once, included Jenna's parents). I'd never heard Lilah being so harsh with Jenna. If your own grandmother doesn't think you're wonderful, who will? We couldn't let this wedding tear us all apart.

Our wine showed up, and I tried to steer the conversation to safer waters. "Lilah, you've had a few, well, more than a few, weddings. What were those like?"

"Well, let's see. Starting backwards. There was the marriage to Ralph about ten years ago, the wedding with the Hawaiian theme in Battle Creek. You were all there for that one." Yes, we were. It would be hard to forget Lilah's geriatric bridesmaids lined up in their grass skirts, shivering in the not-so-balmy Michigan spring. Lilah, however, stole the show with her bodice made from two halves of a coconut. "I don't think you attended the one to Gustav back in '87 in New York. The kids were too little to climb to the top of the Empire State Building, where we had the ceremony." Actually, the kids' mother (that would be me) was too terrified to climb to the top of the Empire State Building. But having young children provides a ready-made excuse to get out of just about anything, doesn't it?

"Gran, just tell us about your first wedding. I intend to have only one in my life."

"We all intend that, Sweet Pea," Lilah said sharply. "But sometimes it just doesn't turn out."

Jenna looked abashed but continued doggedly. "But for the first one, did your father walk you down the aisle?"

"Well, of course he did! He wanted to make sure that I actually got hitched before . . ."

"My dad probably won't even be at my wedding."

"Oh, Jenna, that's not true! Just because Clarisse and I had a minor spat over . . ." Perhaps "minor spat" did not quite describe it. "Minor nuclear meltdown"? But surely that wouldn't prevent Bob from . . .

"No, she's probably right, Angie. I heard that woman whining about it again last night. She has a huge, and I mean huge, influence over him. I'd say the odds of Bob's being there are about nil . . ." I shushed Lilah with a bone-cracking kick this time. I hoped she'd be able to walk again someday.

"The wedding is still a long way off, sweetie. I'm sure they'll change their minds by the time it comes around. Right, Lilah?" Fearing that I might cripple her for life, Lilah nodded emphatically. "Let's talk about other ideas for the wedding. Something fun."

"Like what, Mom?"

"Like, uh, I don't know, like . . ." I signaled the waiter for another round. This was not a chipper little group.

Lilah finally broke the dismal silence. "Well, there's something I've always wondered about. Why on earth do the bride and groom have to stand with their backs to the audience so all you can see is the minister's face? I'd rather see the bride's and groom's faces. Why don't they turn it around? Have the rabbi or minister or priest with their backsides to us. Of course, then recruiting for the cloth would involve different criteria. Like nice-looking rear ends. And you'd also want them to be short so they wouldn't block the view of the happy couple. Yes, you'd definitely want a short pastor with good buns."

"Gran, I want us to face forward."

"Why, Sweet Pea? Afraid you'll be too nervous to look out at the audience?"

"No, because it's traditional."

Lilah and I looked at each other aghast. "Traditional"? Over her lifetime, we'd heard a variety of rationalizations from Jenna explaining why she wanted to do or not do something, but "traditional" had never been one of them. It was clear that something was seriously wrong with our girl.

"Sweet Pea, are you feeling okay? Do you need some recreational drugs to perk you up?"

"Lilah!"

"Not that I have any. I'm just trying to help."

"No, thanks, Gran. I don't use them." Jenna didn't even smile. "I'll be okay." She did not look okay; she looked miserable.

"Hmmm. Well, I'm afraid I have to leave this merry little party and get back over to that woman's house. Angie, would you escort me to the door? I seem to have a nasty bruise on my ankle, and I'm not sure I can walk."

As soon as we were out of earshot, Lilah grabbed my arm and dug all ten fingernails in it. "What is wrong with my granddaughter? I've never seen her like this! Maybe that old man drugged her!"

"What old man?"

"Ryan, of course!"

"Lilah, he's only thirty-seven and . . ."

"Angie Hawkins, that is not the point! Jenna is not acting at all like herself, and she's absolutely miserable! You march back in there and fix it! Bring our Jenna back!" Lilah turned on two very sturdy ankles and stomped out.

Right. Fix it. I returned to the dining room, wondering what the heck I was supposed to do. The only other time I'd lost my real Jenna was in her hormonally charged fifteenth year. After two ugly years of ferocious tantrums, defiant impatience, and unsteady mood swings (Jenna) and the corresponding controlled calm, placid patience, and steady alcohol consumption (me), the sweet, fun girl I had known resurfaced. Certainly we (I?) could get her back again. But perhaps just *being there* for her (and inordinate alcohol consumption) wouldn't be enough this time.

Jenna was studying her binder when I got back to the table. "So Mom, in section six . . ."

"Jenna, let's not get into that just yet. Is something wrong? You don't seem to be quite yourself."

"Ryan said the same thing," Jenna replied, sounding irked. "Now that I'm getting married, I just think that I need to make some changes."

"For Ryan?"

"Well, partially for him, I guess."

"Sweetie, I'm pretty sure Ryan asked you to marry him because he loves you just as you are."

"Maybe. I guess so. It's just that maybe I'm not certain about the whole thing."

"Certain about Ryan?"

"Yes. No. Maybe it's just about getting married itself. I didn't really think about it when I said 'yes.' But since then, it feels like such a big decision to make." Jenna looked up at me desperately. "Mom, why did you marry Dad? How did you know you were ready to get married and that he was The One?"

Uh-oh. My policy with the kids was always as much honesty as I could muster at any point in time. But sometimes the mustering is pretty scary duty.

"Jenna, maybe I'm not a good example of how to pick a husband. No offense to your dad."

"Mom, I know it didn't work out. But you were married for twenty-six years, so something must have been there. Something must have told you that it was right."

There was no squirming out of this one. Here was my precious Jenna, trying to make one of the most critical decisions of her life. It was only fair that she get honest feedback from her mom, however flawed that mom might be.

"Well, Jenna. The truth is that I was pregnant."

"What?" Startled, Jenna spilled an entire glass of Chianti. Wine spilling is actually in her genes as her mother (yes, that would be me) is an accomplished wine spiller. However, if she was planning to follow in my footsteps, she'd have to learn the rules of wine selection as related to tablecloth color. Chianti was definitely not a good choice for the bright white tablecloth that covered our table. But by the traumatized look on her face, I figured that this was neither the time nor place to further her wine-spilling education.

While Jenna and I sopped up the mess, I tried to gather

my thoughts. I signaled the waiter for a refill on Jenna's wine. She was going to need it.

"Okay, Jenna, so let me tell you the whole story. I found out that I was pregnant, and I knew that the father was your dad because he was the only one I was, um, intimate with at the time."

"You and Dad *did it* before you were married?" I could see Jenna was having a hard time with this concept. At age fourteen, Jenna had witnessed me shaking my soccer mom booty in the kitchen to "Layla" (the seventies version, ideal for booty shaking). She had made it very clear at that time that I was "not sexy or cool, had never been sexy or cool, and would never be sexy or cool." Like we all did as young-sters, I'm sure Jenna could not really imagine (and didn't want to imagine) that her parents had sex with each other. She seemed to have accepted my recent dating, and prob-ably the general concept of my being "active." But that's different from accepting the image of your parents as horny twenty-year-olds in the back of a '69 Chevy Cavalier.

"Yes, sweetie, we did. And when I found out that I was pregnant, your dad, to his credit, was ecstatic. But frankly, I didn't know if I wanted to get married."

"Wow. So did you consider abortion?"

Where's the manual for this one? Who told us that one day we would be having discussions with our daughters about whether we've had or considered abortions? And if we had known this discussion was coming up, would we have made different choices?

"I thought about it, but only for an instant. Sweetie, I am in total support of a woman's right to choose whether to have a child or not. But having choice means staying true to yourself, doing what your heart knows is right. And personally, I knew I couldn't have an abortion. It felt like precious life force within me that I couldn't waste."

Jenna looked stunned. Most of us rarely see our parents as being real people, with real dilemmas and imperfect pasts. I doubt the situation itself shocked her as much as the fact that it was good old mom, good old minivan-driving, peanut butter sandwich-making mom, who had been in that situation.

"Sweetie, here's the deal. I was twenty-three, about your age actually, a healthy college graduate from a middle-class family. My family would have been upset about the pregnancy, but they would have stood behind me. Not every woman who unexpectedly finds herself pregnant has that much going for her. So I decided to have the child, the child that turned out to be your brother Tyler."

I looked at Jenna, thirty years behind me in age, and wondered if she could grasp it.

"You must have been frightened, Mom." Yep, she grasped it.

"Yep, Jenna, I was. Anyway, I thought I could just raise the baby by myself. Marrying your dad wasn't really in my thinking. Not that I didn't care for him. But he wasn't, uh, well . . ." Jenna looked at me expectantly. What was the truth here? I sighed remembering. "He wasn't the man of my dreams, Jenna. I had never met that man."

Jenna looked at me sadly, her face plainly revealing her emotional struggle to take this in. Someday, I'd have to teach her my poker face technique.

"But you married Dad anyway?"

I smiled remembering. "Your dad was very persistent, and he talked me into it."

"Oh my gosh! How on earth did he do that?"

"The argument was something like 'Angie, you've always been waiting for the perfect match. But unless you take a chance and try it, how will you know if this is or isn't the perfect match? You might end up on the sidelines your entire life. On the bench. In the stands. Left behind.' Or something like that. Anyway, I decided that I should take my chances with your dad."

"And you stayed with him for twenty-six years based on that proposal?"

"Well, I'm sure hormonal imbalance came into play."

"But, Mom, you must have been totally miserable all those years!"

"Absolutely not! Jenna, I was simply too wonderfully busy to be miserable! I adored Tyler, then you came along, and I adored you, and I enjoyed every minute of your growing. Your dad may not have been very exciting, but he did give me outstanding children. And he was not unkind. The truth is I don't think I expected much out of my relationship with your dad, and I guess I pretty much got what I expected."

Jenna and I looked at each other silently for a few moments. How do you explain all of those subtle, inarticulated decisions you make through the years? The trade-offs? The satisfaction found in an imperfect life?

"Jenna, I wouldn't have traded those years for anything. I have absolutely no regrets that I married your dad. And by the same token, I feel fortunate that he decided to leave after you and Tyler were gone. Does that make sense? Sweetie, everyone writes her own play. Some of us have romance, some of us have none. Some of us have wonderful marriages and no children or children that we hate. Some of us are blessed with children we adore and a mate we can tolerate. There's no perfect path or 'right' road, sweetie. We just give it our best shot and trust. Then accept the consequences of whatever road we choose. Know what I mean?"

Jenna was quiet for a very long time. Her big brown eyes stared at me and her mousey brown hair almost sparkled in the candlelight. She was looking down her own road. And I wondered what she saw.

Chapter 12

After my evening with Jenna, it was official: The only sane being left in my personal universe was me. Everyone else had jumped off the deep end, and it was up to me to bring them back. But how? Unfortunately, I had never progressed beyond dog paddle and I didn't have enough life preservers for all of us. *Being there* was proving to be insufficient for the task; it was time to move into Active Intervention.

I'd always thought of Active Intervention as the activity of busybodies, rabid environmentalists, and the Federal Reserve Board. I basically trust most of us to handle our own lives, and have viewed Active Intervention as suspect, usually annoying, and not always helpful to its recipient. (This, of course, does not apply to Divine Intervention. God and various saints are in charge of Divine Quality Control, so such intervention is more likely to work out in the long run.) So I had avoided it. But desperate times call for desperate measures, and I'd finally hit my most desperate. I spent much of that night trying to figure out what Active Intervention I could use on the soap operas surrounding me.

By that next morning, I was overwhelmed and exhausted, definitely Grade Five. And so I did what I've always done when the world seemed to be falling around my ears: I went to work.

Isn't that what we all do? Not because it's our therapy of choice but because most of us have no choice in the matter. Earning a paycheck requires showing up, no matter what the rest of your life is doing. Your preschooler spikes a fever (you pick him up from day care and install him under your desk in his sleeping bag until you can finish that budget due at 3:00 P.M.). Your sixth-grader chips a tooth at swim practice (you rush her to the dentist, taking that conference call on your cell phone in the dentist's lobby). Your dogs run away rendering your thirteen-year-old hysterical (you console her via phone, call the pound and the SPCA, all the while jamming to finish typing that legal brief). Your boyfriend/husband/significant other leaves you, your period starts unexpectedly with ferocious cramps, the basement floods, your car breaks down—so what? You just grit your teeth and finish that seam, that shift, that class, that patient examination, that payroll run. Is this what we meant when we fought for the right to "have it all"?

I dragged myself into the office and put on my Big Picture Hat to conduct a day of back-to-back conference calls. And, because Big Picture Thinking only requires 13 percent of the average brain (67 percent of brains in average politicians), I was able to discuss Active Intervention methodologies with myself in between asking my Big Picture Questions:

"You're saying that our fire insurance won't cover the water damage from the fire sprinklers? So we should have just let the store burn down to collect?"

Okay, so maybe I've been like those sprinklers, trying to calm Marie down in little squirts. Maybe I need to shoot her with the whole fire hose or add fuel to the fire and let her burn it all up . . .

"If the parking lot is full of potholes, why do we need speed bumps?"

Tyler is too far out of control for speed bumps. I need something to stop him cold. Like those tiger teeth that pop tires! Maybe I could pop Cyndee's boobs and . . .

"So you're telling me that the partners are going to owe capital gains tax on a property that has never made any money and will be sold for less than they paid for it? Is this some kind of new math or what?"

I need to expose Jess to the real math of her new conquests, like when they're in their fifties and still looking like Pierce Brosnan, she'll be ninety-two and looking like one of those dried-apple dolls.

I left the office early. I'd been so weary through the day that I'd barely been able to monotask much less multitask. So how to proceed with Active Intervention was not yet clear, but I felt more encouraged. I just needed a quiet evening to concentrate, organize my thinking, make my lists. And maybe take a little nap.

But my quiet contemplative evening at home was not to be. I drove up in time to see Marie in our mutual driveway, furiously loading a pile of suitcases and boxes into her ancient Land Rover.

"Marie, what's going on?"

"I'm getting out of here before they suck all of the lifeblood out of me." She hefted a box into the trunk with such force that the car shivered in place.

"Who's sucking the lifeblood out of you?"

"Everyone! Jack, the Board, my mother, my daughter. They all want a piece of me. The office expects the impossible on a daily basis. My mom says I don't phone often enough, and my daughter seems to think that I'm her on-call babysitter. And Jack? Jack wants me to be more chipper—more chipper! Can you believe it?"

"Marie, are you feeling quite yourself these days?"

"What self?" she shrieked, terrifying a tree full of magpies. "I'm not a self! I'm a piece of Turkish Taffy getting stretched so thin I could break! No, I'm more like a Cossack tied to four different wild horses, limbs ripping off his body . . ."

"Marie, I don't know about Cossacks or your work or your mother, but I know Jack really loves you."

"And just what do you know of real love?" Marie snapped at me. *That* was a very low blow. Even Marie, in her self-righteous rage, recognized it. She sat on the fender of her car with a despondent sigh and tears in her eyes. "I'm sorry, Angie. I didn't mean it. But I just can't do it all anymore. I can't cope with everything that's coming at me. I've got to get out."

"Out of what exactly?"

"My life."

"Oh, no, Marie! You don't mean . . ."

"No," she said with a sad smile. "Not that. I'm not talk-

143

ing about getting out of life itself, just the life that I'm stuck in. But I really don't know what to do. Or how to even start."

Okay, here was my opening, my big chance for Active Intervention. I just needed to come up with one perfect bit of unsolicited advice, stick my nose full of insightful wisdom in, and badger her into the brilliant suggestion that will cure her. I took a deep breath.

"Marie," I started sincerely, "have you considered getting a tattoo?" Not a brilliant beginning but, hey, I was new at this.

"Angie, why on earth would I get a tattoo?"

"To express your independence and your power. That's what Jenna said about tattoos when she wanted to get one. Of course, she was only fourteen at the time . . ."

"Angie?"

"Yes?"

"Was that supposed to make me feel better?"

"Uh, yes."

"It didn't."

"Oh. Well, then how about a massage? Or a shopping trip to San Francisco?"

"This isn't just the premenstrual blues, Angie. It may sound like it and even feel like it. But I've felt this way for over a month now. There's obviously something seriously wrong with my life."

"But what about Jack?"

"I don't know about Jack. Truthfully, Angie? We haven't had sex in weeks. I thought it was his fault, but it's not. It's me. I'm just not into it." She looked down at her feet forlornly. Of anything she had said so far, this was the most alarming. Could she really have fallen out of love with Jack? I felt as miserable as she looked.

"So, what will you do?"

"I don't know." Marie climbed into her Land Rover and started the engine. "But if I don't get out of here, I'll explode. I'll keep in touch by e-mail." I watched her peel out of the driveway.

Coming through the side gate, I spotted Jack sitting on his back porch, deep in conversation with the pups. Spud rested his head on Jack's thigh and focused his big beagle eyes, full of concern, on Jack's sad face. Alli lay at Jack's feet, snoring in syncopated sympathy. Jack looked so unhappy!

To be honest, I'd been avoiding Jack lately, not knowing what to say or do. Jack is wonderful, funny, and kind. But Marie (who has been none of those things lately) is one of my very best friends. How do I split loyalties? How could I be objective and impartial? The Swiss, with their decades of neutrality, must have some secret for maintaining it. Do you suppose it's in the chocolate? I sat down next to Jack and we shared a few moments of glum silence.

"Angie, have you ever had it all in life? I mean everything you always dreamed about? And then had it explode into nothingness in your face?"

"Um, I think I've had the 'explode in your face' part, Jack, but not the 'everything I've ever wanted' side of it."

"Hmmm. Well, I had everything I ever wanted in Marie. I had love, I had excitement, I had a soul mate."

I was painfully aware of the past tense he used. How could this be happening?

"Perhaps the gods don't like it when a mere human experiences too much happiness. For they've taken it all away." And with that, Jack started to cry.

Geez, I hate it when men cry! Oh, I know they have every bit as much right to cry as women do. Equal opportunity, right? But I've never learned how to handle it well. I grew up with John Wayne and Gary Cooper, stoic guys who were more likely to duke it out with someone than weep.

Women seem to shed tears naturally. Maybe we haven't allowed ourselves enough time for it in the past few decades, but we're still pretty good at crying over both small hurts and big ones. We carry crying supplies, tissue for instance, and we've even developed waterproof mascara to be less ugly when we cry (though with those puffy eyes and red noses, it's unlikely we'll find a way to make weeping glamorous).

But when men cry, I always figure that the agony must be extreme, the situation hopeless. And they are so raw and awkward with it. Maybe it's lack of experience.

I sat next to Jack uneasily, not sure whether to hug him or look the other way until he recovered. In the not knowing, of course, I did neither. Just sat and stared.

"Do you know what she said to me, Angie? She said she would rather wear a burka in Baghdad than live with me anymore."

"Oh, Jack, Marie wouldn't go to Baghdad. She hates the desert and those burkas are so shapeless . . ."

"But she went away, right?"

"Uh, yes."

"Away from me, right?"

"Well, yes, but . . ."

"And we don't know if she's ever coming back, right?"

"Uh . . ." Tears streamed down Jack's face, and my own lower lip started to tremble. "Jack, maybe it isn't as bad as you think."

"Do you really think so, Angie?" Jack sniffled hopefully.

Well, no, actually I didn't really think so. I had never seen Marie like this before, and she seemed determined to leave him along with the rest of her current life. But I wasn't about to say that to poor weeping Jack. Time for Active Intervention: I took a deep fortifying breath and lied through my teeth.

"Of course, I do," I said with trumped-up conviction. "Marie probably just needs some time alone to think about things and, uh, pull herself together. She loves you, Jack. I'm sure she'll be back."

"I hope you're right, Angie. Because I just don't know how I'd go on without her." He started sobbing again, and I sat beside him uncomfortably, making stupid little "there, there" noises and patting his hand.

Chapter 13

I needed some peace and quiet to regroup. But there was obviously no peace to be found at my place that night. So I headed to my sanctuary, the Twenty-ninth Street Gym.

I'm not a natural jock. I would have flunked out of PE in junior high except for the fact that I got extra points for keeping my gym suit clean and correctly identifying intimate body parts by their Latin medical labels. So working out in the get-sweaty-at-a-gym sense had not been part of my lifestyle until a few months ago. At that time, I was trying to get my post-divorce life, including my saggy body, back into shape.

I can't say that I took to weight training gracefully or effortlessly. In fact, I believe the gym took out additional liability insurance after my second session with my personal trainer, Frank. But I swear it was not entirely my fault that the medicine ball got loose and rolled into the Jacuzzi, plugging up the drain and causing a minor flood in the men's locker room and throughout the front lobby.

My regular training nights are Tuesday and Thursday. At the Twenty-ninth Street Gym, these used to be "The Guys" nights, attracting the most serious of weight lifters. I had been adopted as a sort of a mascot, so now those nights were known as "Angie and The Guys" nights. I like it this way because I don't have to compare myself with any slim-waisted, perky-rumped twenty-year-old females while I sweat and grunt. The Guys like it for the comic relief I provide.

The Guys without exception are huge, muscle-bound, and fit. I am not. It took me a while to recognize any of The Guys by name and to figure out that, under all of that unbelievable muscularity, they are individuals. For instance, Keith (the one who rescued me from a runaway treadmill one night) is a police officer. Ralph (who unfortunately once caught my ten-pound weight with his big toe), the lobbyist, introduced me to Jonathan, a pediatrician (who bandaged Ralph's aforementioned weight-catching toe).

The younger Guys had adopted me as their surrogate weight-lifting mom and often asked for motherly advice. I became especially popular during Christmas season as an unofficial shopping consultant.

"Angie, what about a toaster?"

"Okay for a mom. Not okay for a wife or a girlfriend."

"How about a blender? She said she wants a blender."

"Bobby, I don't care what she says. Trust me. If it plugs in, it is not romantic, and you'll be sleeping on the couch."

"So can I get a nightie from Victoria's Secret for my mom? I know she likes that stuff."

"Nope. Too Oedipal."

"Edible?"

"Dude! She means Oedipal like that cat who got it on with his mom."

"No way!"

"Well, yes, but I think Sophocles makes it clear that it was a case of mistaken identity."

"That's sick, Angie. He didn't recognize his own mom? You're shitting me!"

"Watch your language around Angie, dickhead!"

Chivalry is definitely not dead at the Twenty-ninth Street Gym.

Frank, the head trainer at the gym, hadn't arrived yet for my session. I started to warm up with the weights he had bought especially for me (the only weights he could find that were light enough after I'd graduated from twin rolls of toilet tissue). They were bright pink, but Frank had discreetly removed the pink ribbon tassels and Powerpuff Girls stickers. I took my 1.5-pound weights and joined The Guys at the mirror. They all nodded and grunted in greeting, though several shuffled a few safe feet away from me.

"So, guys, let me ask you a question. When a man is crying, what's the right way for a woman to react? I mean, should we put our arms around you or say something? Should we pretend it's not happening, just ignore it?"

There was a dead silence. Everyone froze in place. Embarrassment was thick in the air like a carbon monoxide during a nasty summer traffic jam, similar to the time I walked into the men's shower by mistake. (Hey, sometimes those little universal signs look completely androgynous. How was I to know?) To a man, they avoided eye contact with me and each other. They stared down at their shoelaces, at their knuckles, at their navels. A few even blushed. I had really stepped in it this time. After several agonizing moments, moments even more awkward than watching Jack cry, a deep, strong voice responded from the back of the gym:

"You just be with him, Angie, and let him weep without freaking out." The voice was Tom's, and he walked forward with grace.

Tom does everything with grace. He is maybe sixty or maybe one hundred, it's hard to tell. His leather brown face is lined with a thousand deep wrinkles, and his hair, pulled back in a long ponytail, is pure silver. But his body is strong and supple, and his amazing brown eyes are intelligent and intense. He radiates something like wisdom, though, since wisdom is a pretty scarce commodity, it's difficult to be certain.

Tom was mostly quiet and kept to himself. Our only interaction had been when I'd inadvertently rolled my exercise ball (with me wrapped around it) over him as he was doing sit-ups on the floor. He'd been very gracious about the incident. Frank once told me that Tom is an American Indian and a shaman. I'm not quite sure what a shaman is except I'm pretty sure it has something to do with that grace and wisdom Tom exudes.

"Angie, men feel as deeply as women, but we've been taught to suppress it. In truth, a good cry is very healthy for a man, soul-cleansing."

"So why are we so uncomfortable when men cry?" The Guys were still studying their shoelaces.

"Don't know. Somehow, crying has become miscon-strued as a weakness for men. And maybe that frightens the women around them. But it's not a weakness, Angie. It takes a lot of courage for a man to cry. Truly, it opens the soul to new possibility, renews the masculine spirit."

There was another long pause as the serious shoelace studying continued. The gym was very quiet, with none of the usual clanking of weights and creaking of machines.

"I cried once." Bobby, weighing in at 240 pounds with an *Angels Don't Dare* tattoo, spoke softly. "It was when my dog died. He was a good dog, man." Bobby's eyes turned misty, and his lips trembled.

"My mom died two years ago. She was the best! Re-minds me of you, Angie. Except she weighed more than a house and had bad teeth." Ralph sniffled and rubbed his tear-filled eyes on his sleeve.

"Dude, did you see *Private Ryan?* I went into the john right after that movie and there must've been twenty guys crying at the urinals! I cried too, dude, it was . . ."

"What about game seven of the playoffs in '02? When the Kings gave it away to the Lakers . . ."

"I had this '52 Chevy, man. My dad and I had fixed it up together. It was beautiful! It got totaled by some a-hole on the interstate . . ."

When Frank returned fifteen minutes later, the entire gym was sharing a soul-cleansing, spirit-renewing weeping session while Tom and I doled out tissues and consolation.

"Angie, what the heck is going on here?" Frank bel-lowed. Why does he always leap to the conclusion that everything is my fault?

*   *   *

Jonathan and I walked out of the gym together.

"Would you like a cup of coffee, Angie?" Jonathan is a pediatrician, in his late forties, I think, and definitely on my list of romantic options, though we'd never shared more than a cup of coffee. About six-foot-three with close-cropped steel gray hair, he looks more like a Marine than someone who would spend the day asking toddlers to poke out their tongues.

We stopped at La Bou and Jonathan ordered a "no-foam decaf double latte, extra hot, nonfat." I asked for plain coffee—not particularly suave, but my brain was not up to the task of a more intricate order.

Now why, you are asking yourself, would she order coffee if she's having trouble sleeping? See, the tricky thing about insomnia is that you absolutely cannot sleep when it is appropriate, e.g. when you are home in your cozy bed. But at other times, e.g. when you are out with an attractive man who just might be attracted to you, the eyes get heavy, the limbs become relaxed, the brain fades out . . . With my recent lack of sleep, I would have taken my caffeine intravenously, but that didn't seem to be on the menu.

"That was quite a group therapy session you started in there, Angie."

"All I did was ask a question. It's not my fault if . . ." Jonathan stopped my fervent protest with a smile and a wave of his hand.

"Hey, relax! I think it's great. You add a whole new dimension to that place."

"Class clown?"

"Maybe that, too." I like a man who can be honest, but did he need to be that honest? "But I was talking about the feminine aspect that you bring."

Feminine aspect? Okay, this had more potential. I hadn't had time to give my faltering romantic life much thought lately. Were we leading up to a real date? If so, I could definitely fit it in. I blushed in anticipation. "Well, thanks."

"You know, I was thinking. Would you like to have dinner some evening?"

"Sure. That would be nice." Yippee! Okay, now what will I wear? Do I have time to get my hair colored? Lose that flab on my rear end?

"Good. I'd really like you to meet my partner. He's a great guy, and I think you two would hit it off."

Huh? Oh, maybe this was a work event. "Your partner? Sure, that would be fun. How long have you worked together?"

"Oh, we don't work together. I mean my domestic partner."

Domestic partner? He?

Oh.

If I held three aces and a five with . . .

"Yes. Good. Great. Love to. Sounds swell. Uh, when shall we get together?" I mentally crossed Jonathan off my diminishing list of romantic options.

Chapter 14

To-Do Today:
  Gwen breakfast
  Pick up dry cleaning
  Pick up doggy treats
  Groceries
  Review Budget variance report
  Bank
  Bookstore: <u>Zero Population Growth</u> *(Tyler)*
             <u>Stepford Wives</u> *(Jenna)*
  Lunch Tim
  Dentist appt.

I hadn't seen Gwen since the party in the bridal salon, the merry celebration that evolved into a female version of *Apocalypse Now.* I hardly recognized her waiting for me at our table. Gwen's hair, the shape of which I'd often compared to the Sydney Opera House, was limp and dull. Her typically perfect makeup was fuzzy around the edges, and her elegant suit actually looked wrinkled. She sat slumped in her chair with a row of lipsticks lined up on the table in front of her.

"Gwen? What are you doing?"

"Oh, hi, Angie. I'm just testing for lead poisoning. Jessica told me about an article that says certain lipsticks have toxic levels of lead in them. You can test by coloring a patch of lipstick on your hand, then rubbing with twenty-four-karat gold. If the patch turns black, that lipstick has lead in it. So far, all of these are toxic." I noticed that Gwen wasn't wearing any lipstick at all. My own lips started to itch.

"Gwen, where did Jessica read about this?"

"Oh, some journal or other." I didn't think this was the appropriate time to remind Gwen that Jessica's favorite journals were the *National Enquirer* and *Star.* "I just thought that maybe it would explain why I've been feeling a little vague these days." A little vague wasn't sufficient to describe it. Gwen was acting as if she had about half of her normal IQ, like a computer stricken with a nasty virus or maybe an insidious worm. (Not that I know the difference between a computer worm versus a computer virus or how to cure either one. Starve a virus, feed a worm?)

A waiter approached our table. Upon seeing Gwen, he gasped, clutched his heart, stumbled, and turned quickly as if to flee. His reaction was not uncommon; Gwen in her normal state is the terror of the restaurant community. She likes what she likes, exactly as she likes it—and she makes it very clear. Unfortunately, what she likes is seldom on the menu, but that never deters her from asking for it. Rumor has it, the restaurant union is negotiating hazard pay for employees working in restaurants Gwen frequents. I smiled reassuringly at the waiter, whose name tag revealed him to be George, and ordered my scrambled eggs quickly.

"And for you, miss?" he turned to Gwen with a look of a condemned man.

"Oh, I'll just have the same," she replied.

George waited; I waited. Finally, Gwen looked up from her lipsticks with a puzzled expression on her face.

"Is that okay? I'll just have whatever she ordered."

"Uh, certainly, miss. Nothing else?" George and I waited with bated breath. (Bated is the fourteenth-century short version of abate and means to hold back, in case you were wondering. Just an example of the useless knowledge I had gained from hours of reading the dictionary in the middle of my sleepless nights. . . . Mighty Manfred the Wonder Dog, Tom Terrific, Captain Kangaroo, Mr. Green Jeans . . .)

"No, thank you."

"You don't want Armenian bread with the crusts cut off, toasted on just one side?" George inquired anxiously.

"No."

"You don't want your juice freshly squeezed with extra pulp on the side?" George's voice rose with a tinge of hysteria.

"No, I . . ."

"You don't want your eggs from free-range, corn-fed chickens who . . ."

I cut him off firmly before he lost all self-control and

threw himself on the butter knife. "Really, that's all she wants today," I intervened. "Thank you, George."

Like a slap in the face, this brought George back from the brink. He looked at me in wonderment and turned dazedly to the kitchen.

I looked for my opportunity to Actively Intervene with Gwen. "Gwen, have you been to see a doctor lately?" Normally such a comment to Gwen would have earned me a severely raised eyebrow and a caustic remark. Today, it earned me nothing.

"He says it's probably stress, maybe burnout. But that can't be it. I've cut way back on work. I'm barely working sixty hours a week, and I took a day off just last month." Gwen's idea of a light workload and mine are quite different. "But he took some blood tests anyway." She paused and looked pensive. "Maybe I've just used it all up."

"Used what all up?"

"My brain, my intellect, my ability to think."

"Like a box of tissues?"

"Yes, or maybe it's just gone stale, old, and moldy, like a loaf of bread."

"Gwen, I don't think . . ."

"Or like a sponge that sits in the sink and gets full of germs and stinks so you have to throw it away."

"Gwen, you're not going to throw away . . ."

"Maybe being brilliant is all over for me, Angie. I used too much of my brainpower at the front end of my life and now, there's none left."

"Honestly, Gwen, I don't think the brain works like that."

"But you don't know for sure, do you Angie?"

Well, yes, lacking credentials in neurology I really couldn't say for sure. "Gwen, it can't be that bad. You must be exaggerating."

"Ha! You think I'm exaggerating? Come with me to court this morning, Angie, and you'll see how bad it is."

"Oh, I couldn't, Gwen. I've got a full day planned and . . ."

"It's just a prehearing. Only forty-five minutes at the most. Please, Angie, I could really use your support." Gwen looked at me pleadingly, a look that is so very un-Gwen-like.

"Okay," I said reluctantly, and headed to the lobby to use my cell phone to rearrange my day.

"Psst!"

I looked around to see our waiter George gesturing wildly.

"This way!" he whispered. I followed him into a small corridor. He looked furtively over his shoulder.

"Miss, your friend, there's something definitely wrong with her."

"Tell me about it."

"Not that I actually preferred her when she was herself."

"I know what you mean."

"But she was a very good tipper. Anyway, don't you think you could do something about it? Bring her back to herself? You seem like the kind of friend who can fix things."

"I do?"

"Yes, I can tell by your shoes."

"My shoes?"

"Yes. They are very practical. Naturalizers, right?"

"Ah. So you trust me to retrieve my friend from the brink of insanity based on my choice of shoes?"

"Yes," George said, all seriousness and sincerity.

"I'm working on it. I'll let you know how it goes."

"Don't tell the union I've asked you to do this. They might consider it disloyal."

"I'll keep it quiet."

Returning to the lobby, I called Tim and got his voice mail.

"Hi, Tim. It's Angie. I hope you get this message. Something has come up and I can't join you for lunch. I'm, uh, free tomorrow night though, so if you want, we can do something then. Okay? Well, okay then. I'll try to call you later."

The hearing was in front of Judge Masters, who by all accounts would have been called a "hanging judge" if hanging were an option in civil matters. (It is rumored that he thought it should be and hoped to institute the Three Strikes penalty for repeat jaywalking offenders). Apparently, he used to sit on the criminal court bench, but had been moved to civil court after a few of his "seventy lashes" sentences had to be overturned.

Judge Masters looked like a cross between Karl Malden and Lurch. His natural expression was of a man unexpectedly swallowing sour milk, and clearly his sense of humor had been surgically removed at birth. I doubt he's ever been described as a "fun kinda guy."

Gwen shuffled her papers nervously as Judge Masters settled himself in his seat. Gwen's client, a middle-aged woman in a well-tailored business suit, looked at Gwen anxiously.

"The plantiff will make the opening statement. Ms. Winsor?"

"Uh, yes. Um, let's see. Your Honor." Gwen stood hesitantly, biting her lower lip. "Uh, my client the defendant . . . no, I'm sorry, I mean the plaintiff. Anyway, we want to tell the court that, um . . ." Gwen's client looked amazed and alarmed. The young defense attorney sitting at his table across the aisle smirked maliciously.

This was awful! My articulate, feisty, brilliant Gwen sounded like Elmer Fudd playing Daffy Duck. I offered as much silent support as I could. *C'mon, Gwen! You can do this!*

I saw a documentary once on psychokinesis. People made pencils skitter across tables and spoons bend slowly into odd shapes without touching them at all, using only mental concentration. I honestly think there are more efficient methods for pencil moving and spoon bending, but perhaps I could use psychokinesis to jump-start Gwen's brain.

I took a deep breath and concentrated as ferociously as I could. *Gwen*, my mind shouted to her mind. *You are smart! You are brilliant! You can do this!* I was giving myself a headache. Gwen turned around and looked at me quizzically for an instant. Maybe she was getting the vibes! I concentrated harder in a pose not unlike that of someone having a difficult bowel movement.

"So, Your Honor, when my, uh, client, went to that, um, place, she took the thingy . . ."

The judge stared at Gwen, mesmerized by her performance. "The 'thingy,' Ms. Winsor?"

"Yeah, uh yes, Your Honor. The thingy that you file when you . . ."

Gwen's ship was going under fast. My psychic support was doing no good. Perhaps I should have started with spoons and worked up to brains. But I still had to save my friend! I couldn't let her be humiliated like this. I had to Intervene.

"I object!" I yelled from my seat.

There was a stunned hush as Judge Masters surveyed the sparse audience to see who dared to create such an inappropriate disturbance in his courtroom. A woman sitting next to me leaned away and pointed at me. What a snitch!

"Madam, who might you be?"

"Angie. Angie Hawkins, Judge, Your Honor, sir."

"And what interest do you have in this case?"

"Well, none exactly. I'm just a concerned public citizen."

"I see. Well, Ms. Hawkins, I suggest you keep your concerns to yourself, or I will have you evicted from the proceedings. Do I make myself clear?"

"Um, I think so. So you're saying that if I say something . . ."

"Ms. Hawkins! Be quiet!"

"Oh. Okay." He glared at me.

"So as you were saying, Counselor?"

"Well, Your Honor, my client was proceeding to the office of the defendant when . . ." Good! My disturbance seemed to have brought Gwen to herself like a dash of cold water. She was on a roll, talking confidently and using polysyllabic words again. Pleased with myself, I relaxed into my seat. However, it didn't take long for Gwen's boat to start leaking again. "And then the, uh, guy, that guy who does the, you know, the stuff with those papers when you get a job . . ."

"The HR manager?" Judge Lurch prompted.

"That's correct, him. Well, when this lady . . ." Gwen pointed to the woman seated beside her.

"Ms. Jenkins? Your client?"

"Yes, her. She, uh . . ." Gwen looked blank and stared at the desk. There was an excruciating silence. The judge stared; Gwen's client covered her face with her hands; the defense attorney smirked again; and Gwen's eyes started to tear up. It was too painful to bear.

"Objection!" someone hollered from the audience. We all looked around to see who had done it. Uh-oh. Turns out it was me.

The judge looked up angrily, a big vein in his neck pulsating noticeably, and stared straight at me. "Ms. Hawkins, you were warned."

"Oh, I'm so sorry, Your Honorary Justice, sir. I just got caught up in the moment and . . ."

"Bailiff, remove this public citizen from the courtroom!" The bailiff moved toward me.

It was one of those slow-motion moments; everything and everyone moved at half speed like an underwater ballet. As the big chunky guy with the clunky gun belt and the badge oozed toward me, I frantically racked my pathetic sleep-deprived brain to come up with a plan. I couldn't leave Gwen like this. She said the hearing would be forty-five minutes, and there were only fifteen minutes left. If I could only stall long enough . . . But what could I do to stall?

Suddenly scenes from my college days came back to me. I was in school during the Vietnam, Cambodia years, the years of war protests. We had staged sit-ins and walkouts, candlelight vigils, and fasts. It was nonviolent civil protest and, if nothing else, it did take up a lot of time.

As the bailiff approached, I folded my arms and looked straight ahead. "What are you doing?" Gwen mouthed silently at me. I wrapped my arms under the armrests to anchor myself to the seat. The cowardly snitch-woman next to me moved out of the row to give the bailiff access.

"Come with me, ma'am," the bailiff said, towering over me. I shook my head. "Ma'am, I need to ask you again to please stand up and come with me." I shook my head again. To give myself courage, I started humming, rocking back and forth in my chair. Not remembering any of our protest songs, I hummed "Jingle Bells"; it worked just as well. *Dashing through the snow . . .*

The bailiff looked helplessly at the judge. Gwen motioned me to get up. Nope. *O'er the fields we go . . .*

"Bailiff, go get some assistance to lift that woman up bodily and get her out of here! You will be charged with contempt of court, madam. This case will be postponed and recalendared." The judge slammed his gavel, a little harder than necessary I thought, and stomped out of the courtroom. What a grouch! Maybe he suffered from ulcers.

The courtroom cleared. Gwen mouthed to me "I'll bail you out," as she exited with her hysterical client. My mission accomplished, I stood meekly to accompany the five well-armed bailiffs who arrived to escort me out.

Jingle all the way . . .

Chapter 15

My body felt thoroughly anesthetized through the tedious intake procedure. Me, who had received A's in elementary school for good citizenship, me who had never even been in detention in high school, me who had voted in every election, taken my daily vitamins, and even showed up for all of my regularly scheduled mammograms . . . this same me was now headed up the river! (Well, not actually up the river; the jail was right across the street from the courthouse and next to the lot where I'd left my car. I assumed they weren't going to validate my parking.) Prior to that moment, my rap sheet had consisted of exactly one parking ticket in 1988 written by an overzealous meter maid. I had always been a perfect child, perfect student, perfect citizen.

That wasn't because I aspired to sainthood or because I was intrinsically virtuous. I was just terrified of getting in trouble. I envied those kids who pushed the limits, but I wasn't one of them. Even in the late sixties when I joined the war protesters, we had kids who planned to get arrested and those who didn't. I was always one of those who didn't.

So what could have possibly possessed me in that courtroom? Well, actually I knew exactly what possessed me. It was a combination of loyalty and Grade Six sleep deprivation. I couldn't sit by idly and watch one of my best friends humiliate herself, and I didn't have enough time or brainpower to come up with a better plan.

They took my belt, my purse, and my shoes (obviously concerned that I might pummel myself to death with my Naturalizers). The matron walked beside me in my jailhouse muff-muffs, down the corridor and into my cellblock. How many people do you know who have their own cellblock? Yeah, me neither.

Even the most enthusiastic of real estate agents would have a hard time describing the jailhouse as "light and airy," "full of old world charm," or "cute and cozy." The ambience was more accurately described as Postmodern Dismal, with its dirty khaki-colored walls and its lighting as dreary as a discount store dressing room. Twenty odd cells banked the cold, broad corridor; some were larger, to accommodate a few women, and others were smaller and held just one. The matron led me to one of the smaller cells at the far end.

"Here you go, Hawkins. Being new to this system, you might prefer a little privacy."

New to this system? Like this was orientation for the future? My emotional state advanced from dazed to depressed, and as soon as the matron left the catcalls started.

"Yo! Sweetie Pie!"

"Oooo, we got ourselves a little Junior League Lady now."

Most of the jeers came from the cell directly across from me, a larger space housing four or five women of various shapes and sizes. I didn't look closely enough to get much detail (surely staring would be rude even in a jail cell!) but I got the distinct impression that these were not the ladies on our church social planning committee. Maybe if I just ignored them, they'd get bored and leave me alone. I flopped myself onto the cot which, due to its singular lack of padding, was not a good idea. I'd had a lot of not-good ideas lately.

"Bring out the tea and cookies. We got us a real fancy-pants princess."

"So what are you in for, Baby Cakes? Disrupting a Tupperware party?"

I felt like a monkey in a cage at the zoo. There was nowhere to hide, not even a little fake rock or shrub to sit behind. And I was starting to feel that perhaps my jailers had placed my cage a little too close to the lions' den. Intellectually, I knew I was safe—wasn't I?—but I still felt edgy. Those lions looked pretty mean and hungry; my one cardio-kickboxing class had focused on minimizing the gluteus maximus, not on self-defense.

"No, she looks like she did some serious jaywalking. Maybe with her little pink poodle . . ."

"My, my, my, aren't we lucky? We've got our own little Miss Martha Stewart . . ."

And that's when I lost it.

"That's it!" I roared, leaping up from my cot. "I've had enough! I hate Martha Stewart! Well, not Martha Stewart, the person per se, but everything she stands for! Dammit! Who on earth makes marshmallows from scratch, I ask you? That woman is sick, and I refuse to be compared to her!"

"Well, little missy . . ."

"Don't you 'little missy' me!" I grabbed the bars of my cell and shook them violently. (In case you need to know for future reference, shaking cell bars violently does not actually move the bars at all. But it certainly realigns the spine.) I glowered ferociously at my tormentors and continued to scream out my frustration. "I've had a hell of a time lately, and I don't need any flak from you! Marie goes off the deep end and wants to bludgeon her perfectly good husband to death. And she has no desire for sex, which is so unlike Marie I just can't tell you. And then Jessica starts chasing after men half her age and is totally horny and out of control, twitchy and jittery. Not that Jess hasn't always been a little off . . ."

"Well, maybe . . ."

"Don't interrupt! I'm not finished!" I bellowed. This was beginning to feel really good! Much better than pounding on a pillow or taking deep breaths or counting to ten. I let loose, and yelled so loudly that my words echoed down the corridor. "My daughter announces that she's getting married to a guy who is closer to my age than hers and dyes her hair brown—ugly, ugly brown!—and turns into one of the Stepford wives—not those funny ones but the scary ones! Then my son's girlfriend, who has the intelligence of

169

broccoli and boobs the size of watermelons—no, maybe more cantaloupes, or is it casaba melons? Which are those green ones?"

By then my audience was rapt, or perhaps stunned speechless, and no one dared to answer. "Anyway, this floozy wants to use my son as a stud and have his baby to beautify the gene pool. Can you believe it? And to top it all off, my brilliant friend Gwen loses every brain cell she ever had which is why I'm here because I had to intervene for her in court to preserve her self-esteem! So dammit! Don't you little missy, Martha Stewart, sweetie pie me!"

Completely out of steam, I collapsed on the floor with my head in my hands. Catharsis feels good but is certainly exhausting (How many calories do you suppose I burned off?) Maybe if I kept my eyes closed long enough, I would wake up from this really awful dream. There was a long eerie silence throughout the cellblock. Did everybody go home?

"So are you here on a homicide charge?" I looked up. The woman who spoke was tall and slim, dressed in muted slacks and a professional-looking blouse. "Whatever the charge, I think you've got a pretty good case for an insanity plea."

"The Professor should know, *chica*. She's a doctor," commented a small, sturdily built Hispanic woman in flashy, skintight orange dress.

"Of philosophy," the Professor clarified.

"No, I didn't kill anybody," I said with a sigh. "It's contempt of court. Maybe resisting arrest, I'm not quite sure."

"What be your name, hon?" asked a very large black woman in a flamboyant red jumpsuit.

"Angie. Angie Hawkins."

"Well, Angie Hawkins, you jest as well tell us da' whole story. We got plenty o' time to kill, and dey don't got no *Oprah* in here."

So I told them the whole story: Gwen, nasty Judge Masters, the smirk of the defense attorney, "Jingle Bells."

"You know I believe I remember Masters. Cantankerous old guy?" the Professor remarked. "Looks as though he has a chronic duodenal ulcer? Whenever he gets really frustrated, a big vein in his neck starts throbbing. Did you get that vein to throb?"

"Um, yes, I guess I did."

"Excellent, Angie!"

"You da' man, babe! Well, Angie Hawkins, looks like we got us a sitch-oo-ation here, huh?"

"You got that right, DeeDee. This poor little *chica* is in way over her head."

"So what do y'all think? I'm thinking it be menopause. Professor?"

"Well everything she has said thus far indicates . . ."

"What are you talking about?" I said. "I'm not menopausal. I just had my period and . . ."

"Not you, Angie. Those friends of yours. What were their names? Gwen, Jessica, and Mary? They are exhibiting classic perimenopausal symptoms."

"Uh, it's Marie. They are?"

"Of course. Take for instance, the one who is unreasonably angry and not interested in sexual activity."

"*Sí, sí!* My tia Rosa was going through the change, you know? Some stupid john tried to get into her skirts, you know? So she took the knife to his *huevos*. Now he sings like an f-ing soprano."

My Spanish isn't good but I was pretty sure Tia Rosa hadn't cut up someone's breakfast. "Uh, so what happened to Rosa?"

"Oh, she got twenty years. But then they gave her some *remedio* in the joint so she don't get crazy and cut up the guards. She feels real good now."

"Oh, well, that's, uh, nice. I'm glad she's feeling better." And no longer has access to sharp objects.

"And then, Angie, there's your friend whose libido level has risen to obsessive levels . . ."

"Unh-huh. Let me tell you on that one," DeeDee broke in excitedly. "My girlfriend, see? She thinks I don't know when she hits on every young skirt what hits the street. But I know'd. She say she jest can't help it. Turns out she telling true, she's got that men-o-pause thing. But I beat the sh-t outta all her cutesy girlfriends anyhow. Unh-huh. Now she on some hor-o-mones and she be back to being faithful. Only now I got to do some time for doing that beating . . ."

"Oh, gosh! Wow, that's too bad, DeeDee. I'm so sorry. But you, uh, had the best intentions. I mean, you couldn't have known, right?" I always try to be polite, but what is the politically correct response to such revelations? It was becoming clear that my cellblock mates were not here for traffic violations.

"Yo! But what about that stupid one? The one with *chorizo* for brains?"

"Gwen? She's not stupid; she's brilliant. At least she was brilliant until a few weeks ago."

"And let me guess," commented the Professor. "Now she can't handle complex mental activity or string two thoughts together. She forgets things easily and perhaps she's more emotional than usual."

"That's it exactly! How did you know?"

"Because I experienced the very same symptoms. I researched it in several medical journals and realized I needed some form of hormonal supplement. I had to experiment with a few before I felt the effects. But finally my brain kicked back in gear, and I was able to pull off the best con of my career."

"Hey, if it be the best con of your career, Professor, how come you in the joint again?"

"I was with my significant other when he got a parking ticket."

"That doesn't seem fair!" I huffed indignantly, outraged by the unfairness of the judicial system. "You're in jail because of a parking ticket? A parking ticket that wasn't even yours?"

"The ticket wasn't mine, but then again, the car wasn't his either."

"Oh. I see. I guess the authorities don't appreciate that type of thing, do they?"

"No, Angie, they don't."

We talked about menopause some more, everyone

telling their stories. Other women along the cellblock threw in their comments, and it felt like the awkward seating of a long banquet table. All I could see of the people down the row were pairs of hands gesturing through their bars: white hands, black hands, brown hands, and yellow hands. Small hands, large hands; some were coarse and manlike, others were feminine with bright polished nails. This conversation definitely gave new meaning to the phrase "talk to the hands."

Everyone had a story, most of which did not end happily ever after with the charming prince and princess riding off into the sunset. In these stories, the princess was more likely to yank the prince off his high horse and pummel him soundly, stealing whatever princely jewels he had in his saddlebags. (Honestly, someone should do a serious research project on the connection between hormonal imbalance and crime rates. Free dispensation of hormone replacement therapies might reduce the female prison population substantially.) Finally, we ran out of menopause stories.

"But what about my daughter Jenna? She's definitely not acting like herself. And she's way too young for menopause."

"You know what Kierkegaard said?" the Professor mused. " 'The greatest hazard of all, losing one's self, can occur very quietly in the world, as if it were nothing at all. No other loss can occur so quietly; any other loss—an arm, a leg, five dollars, a wife, etc.—is sure to be noticed.' "

The entire cellblock observed a respectful moment of silence, absorbing this thought.

"Angie's girl ain't losing herself, Professor. She just gettin' married. You gotta change when you get married, you know? It's just the way it is."

"No way!"

This started a spirited debate among my fellow prisoners that would have made Gloria Steinem proud. A few made the case for traditional women's roles based on preserving the family unit (though I never quite grasped how grand theft auto was supposed to fit within that picture). Others argued for the importance of women remaining independent and having fulfilling careers to enhance their life experience. (Unfortunately, most of the life-enhancing careers chosen by this group fell in the felony category.)

"Well, I'm never lettin' no hairy, tobacco-chewing, beer-swilling pair o' pants make me change!"

"That's 'cuz you like girls, DeeDee."

"That make no difference. I know'd who I am. Anybody wants to be with me better damn well like me just like I is!"

"You feel that way, DeeDee, because you have a healthy dose of self-esteem. Maybe that's her daughter's problem. Maybe she's lacking in self-esteem," the Professor posited.

"Jenna? Oh, I don't think so. At least, she never showed signs of it before this."

"Then you know what I be thinkin', Angie Hawkins? I think your little girl be just fine. Give her time. She'll come back around. You finally did, right?"

"Well, yes, but it took me twenty-six years."

"Some of us are a little slower than others, Angie."

"But what about Tyler? Will he come around, too? Cyndee seems to have him hopelessly ensnared. I have no idea how to fix that one."

The entire cellblock cracked up with laughter.

"That be the easiest of all, *chica*. You just off the *perra fea!*"

"If you need any referrals to appropriate resources, Angie, you just let us know."

"Uh, thanks."

Hours later, I was still sitting in that cell. Our spirited and enlightening cellblock discussion had eased into companionable silence. I heard a familiar voice greeting the other prisoners. I'd always seen him in his gym attire; his pressed slacks and crisp, long-sleeved shirt made him look quite different. But his long silver ponytail and graceful walk made him instantly recognizable.

"Hi, Tom," I ventured meekly. Now that my latest explosion had passed and I'd spent a few hours behind bars, my natural state of meek was returning.

"Angie? What on earth are you doing here?" For the first time ever, I saw astonishment on Tom's normally impassive face.

"Oh, just doing a little time," I said, feeling a couple of tears slip down my cheek. "What about you?"

"I counsel the inmates. Angie, how did you get here?"

So I explained the whole story: the kids, my friends, the judge with the throbbing vein and no sense of humor. My cellblocks mates threw in a few colorful comments and their vehement opinions. Tom seemed to think their insights and suggestions were pretty good, except for the offing Cyndee plan.

"Perhaps a higher quality substitution would be a better strategy, Angie."

"Yeah, Tom, we gotta find Angie's kid a chick with better hooters."

"Perhaps." Tom smiled. "But, Angie, why didn't you call someone to set bail for you?"

"I thought Gwen would get me out. I used my one phone call to cancel my dental appointment."

Tom shook his head and stared at me in amazement. "Okay, look, we'll get you another phone call. Do you know whom you can call?"

I thought of Gwen. Nope, too unreliable. Marie? Jessica? Nope. All of the friends I would have trusted in the past had become completely unpredictable. Even Jenna was goofy. Tyler was my only hope.

Tom and the matron escorted me to the phone room and we quickly connected to Tyler. Explaining it all to Tyler, I made it to the part about the courtroom bailiff coming to haul me away. But then I crumpled, choking on my tears. Tom took the phone and calmly told Tyler the rest of the story and explained what needed to be done.

On the way back to my cell, Tom put his arm through mine and my tears really started to flow. Isn't it the way? When you're in trouble, you can hold it together completely and be tough. But as soon as someone shows you a little warmth and kindness, all of your toughness dissolves into a puddle.

"Angie, you've been worrying a lot about all of this, haven't you?"

"Uh-huh."

"You know, when you fill your mind with worry and fear, you block the answers you seek and the good from getting to you."

"You do?"

"Yes. The Universe has everything you need and is willing to offer it to you, Angie. But it's like a garden hose. If you step on that hose, with too much worry and too much fear, the water can't get through."

"It can't?"

"No, it can't. You have to relax, let go and trust a little so that it will flow."

"Hmmm. I guess I can give it a try, Tom. Is this one of the mystical teachings of shamanism?"

"Nope. I think I got this one from a fortune cookie."

My cellblock mates and I had passed the time talking about family (I had a lot to contribute), lovers (I had very little to contribute) and our criminal histories (I kept my mouth shut). We also spent a good part of the time talking about our marriages. (Divorce is rampant in California, but I don't think this group contributed much to the statistics. Their unfaithful, insensitive, or abusive spouses were more likely to end up as missing persons on the sides of milk cartons.) I taught them how to make origami cranes out of notebook paper and wrote out copies of Clarisse's recipe for Double Chocolate Cream Cheese Brownies for everyone.

Tyler and his boss Eric showed up around four-thirty. Eric, a very good-looking attorney in his fifties, had been number three on my list of romantic options. (I'll bet *The Rules* would discourage asking potential dates to set bail for you.) Eric and I had been on one semidate together, attending his office party about a month ago. This semidate hadn't been terribly exciting and, honestly, I found Eric to be fairly boring. But a man with looks that rival George Clooney's should always be given a second chance, right?

Tyler and Eric were waiting for me at the counter in the lobby of the jail. Eric's face had a distinct look of disapproval, his lips ready to "tut-tut." He reminded me of those old codgers who look like they're sucking on lemons and keeping moral report cards on the rest of us. Despite his good looks, Eric is definitely on the brink of old coot-dom.

Tyler, on the other hand, walked up and put his arms around me protectively, looking concerned but calm and nonjudgmental. I'm pretty sure this was the very same look I gave him many years ago when I was called to his preschool because he had an "accident" in his overalls.

"Are you okay, Mom?"

"Yes, honey, I'm fine. Thank you both for coming."

"I talked to Judge Masters. He said he would drop the charges if you promise never to show up in his courtroom again." Eric sounded impatient and supercilious. It's hard to be grateful to a knight in shining armor who sneers at you after the rescue. I mentally zapped Eric off my list.

"Thank you, Eric. I really appreciate it."

"I explained to him you had some issues, that it was a female thing, time of the month, and all that." Eric looked quite pleased with himself. "That usually shuts them right up and handles it."

A female thing? Time of the month? He made it sound

like a form of insanity. Which, make no mistake, it can be. But while women can talk about our "female things" that way, it's obnoxiously patronizing coming from a man. I felt another rant gathering in my breast.

"Angie." Tom appeared from nowhere, with his calm voice and smiling eyes. His firm hand on my arm cut off my latest eruption before it spewed forth. "Is this your son?"

I swallowed the urge to clobber Eric and introduced my son. Tom grasped Tyler's hand and looked deeply into his eyes. Tyler gazed back at him, calmly and with confidence. After a few moments, they both grinned. Obviously a guy thing.

"Tyler, why don't you join your mom at the gym Thursday night? Meet some of her other friends."

"I'll do that, Tom. And thank you very much for taking care of my mother."

"From what I hear from her cellblock mates, your mom can take pretty good care of herself, son." Tom gave me a hug and left.

After the paperwork was done and my shoes returned to me, Tyler and I retrieved my car. (Just as I suspected, the jail does not validate parking.) As we drove home, he held my hand.

"Mom, what's going on?"

So I explained to him about the aunties and hormones, craziness and libido, Kierkegaard and *huevos*. He looked a little queasy but, to his credit, listened carefully and asked intelligent questions.

"So what are you going to do, Mom? Can I help?"

"Maybe if you could just check in with Jenna, honey."

And ditch that conniving girlfriend of yours before I have to intervene with my "resources" to do the job.

"We're double-dating tomorrow night. I'll talk to her. But what about the aunties?"

"I think I've figured out what their problem is, honey. I just need to come up with a good plan."

Chapter 16

That night when I returned home from my encounter with the penal system, I found I couldn't (surprise, surprise!) sleep. So I got on the Internet, which also never sleeps, and looked up menopause. My search brought up 1,101,331 sites. I guess menopause has become big business with all of us Baby Boomers bursting into it. There's even an International Menopause Society, probably with elaborate ceremonies and a secret handshake.

I found medical information, chat rooms, poetry sites (who would have thought to rhyme Santa Claus with menopause?)—more information than anyone could possibly absorb in one night. But I did get some of the basics down and realized that my friends' symptoms were all there: increased libido, decreased libido, rage, inability to think clearly. "The Change" sounded more like a journey into psychosis than a gentle transition into our elder years. (It's a traitorous thought, but when we do finally get a woman president, I certainly hope she's passed through menopause already or has extraordinary medical support. On the other hand, our male presidents have been acting irrationally for over two hundred years with no hormonal excuse at all. A little menopause madness would hardly be noticeable.) I learned that perimenopause is the beginning stage when hormones are zipping around out of control, causing the first symptoms to appear. Menopause is the stage when these hormones stabilize. Could this mean Gwen would stabilize as a moron, Marie as a bitch, and Jess as a cradle robber?

Around four in the morning, I stumbled across a seminar titled *Menopause, the Next Frontier* to be given by a local naturopath the next evening. Perfect! But how to get them all there? I had a sneaking suspicion that my three hormone-zipping friends would not be thrilled to attend. I came up with a perfect plan (though plans considered perfect at 4:00 A.M. often seem less so at 9:00 A.M. the next day). I created the bait, sending this e-mail to each one of them, individualizing with slight variations in the text:

> *Hi, Gwen/Marie/Jessica!*
>
> *Guess what? I've been given two front-row tickets to see Yo-Yo Ma/Wynton Marsalis/Yanni in concert tomorrow night. Meet me on front steps of the Community Center at 7:00 PM.*

I hit the SEND button with hope in my heart and hit the sack with exhaustion in my limbs.

Having lost so much time per my jaunt in the jailhouse, I spent the next day frantically catching up at work. Petunias or pansies? Coke machines or Pepsi machines? Horizontal or vertical blinds? With so many critical decisions to make on so little sleep, perhaps it's understandable that it wasn't until 5:15 P.M. that I remembered to call Tim to break our date. He answered on the first ring, as if waiting for my call.

"Tim, I hate to do this again, but I'm afraid I can't see you tonight. Something has come up."

"Something has come up?" By his voice, I don't think he was smiling.

"Um, yes, with Jessica, Gwen, and Marie." Tim was silent, waiting for further explanation. But what could I say? I'm dragging the three of them to a menopause seminar to save their sanity and mine?

"I see. This seems to be happening a lot lately, Angie."

"I know. I'm sorry it's just . . ."

"And it seems like the more I want to be around, the less available you've become."

"Tim, it's not that. They just need me right now."

"Seems like they always need you. Maybe you need to choose, Angie. Between them and me."

What was he saying? Choose? Let's see: my family and my friends of twenty years versus a man I'd met six months ago? The women who had seen me through childbirth, divorce, and the worst haircut I've ever had, versus a guy with a killer smile and no patience?

"I'm sorry, Tim."

"Oh. I guess that's it then," and Tim hung up the phone.

I put the receiver down slowly. I had done the right thing. I knew it was the right thing. I couldn't have done anything else, could I? All right, so my list of potential romantic options was down to nil. But so what? Plenty of attractive, middle-aged fish in the sea, right? Besides, with both of my kids in turmoil, my friends prime candidates for the county asylum, and my body refusing to sleep, who had the time or energy to pursue a romantic relationship? Even if I did, who needed Tim anyway?

So why were those tears dribbling down my cheeks?

Being new to Active Intervention, I am perhaps better at *planning* the perfect plan than *executing* the perfect plan. By the time I left the office, dashed home to feed the pups, cleaned up the mascara rivulets on my face, drove back downtown, and found a parking space, I was late. I found my three best friends (who had not been late and therefore had time to compare notes and work themselves into a fury) looking like a lynching party on the Community Center steps. Apparently, I was to be the lynchee.

"Angie! What the heck is this all about?" Jessica stomped her size six foot in its bizarre looking platform shoe.

"Yo-Yo Ma is not playing tonight, Angie. Neither is Yanni or Winston Marsalis," Gwen said angrily.

"That's Wynton," Marie corrected.

"Who's Wynton?"

"Marsalis."

"Oh," said Gwen, suddenly unsure of herself. "So is he here?"

"Gwen! Pay attention! Angie has obviously tricked us into coming to this . . . this . . . seminar."

"You've done some pretty strange things over the years, Angie. But this is the strangest. Why would you bring us here? To a menopause seminar of all things!" Marie demanded angrily.

"Look, I'm sorry I tricked you. But all three of you have been acting so unlike yourselves lately. And I really think that maybe you are all going into menopause. Or maybe perimenopause. See, it all fits perfectly. Gwen's vagueness in the head, Marie's mood swings, Jessica's formiculation . . ."

"Well, I never!" Jess huffed. "I'll admit I've been getting around a bit lately but . . ."

"No, for-mic-u-la-tion. That thing where you feel ants crawling all over you. It's one of the classic symptoms."

"Angie, this is ridiculous." Gwen raised her eyebrow, a visage of her old arrogant self. "Even if one of us, and I'm not saying which one, was entering menopause, what are the odds that all three of us would go into it at exactly the same time?"

"Well," Marie ventured, "I suppose it could be like those studies where college girls in the same dorm start cycling their menstrual cycles together . . ."

"Or," Jess contributed, "it might be that the moon is in a particular phase of feminine activity that is drawing the yin . . ."

"No! It's none of that!" I interrupted vehemently. "It's that we're all between the ages of forty-five and fifty-five which is statistically when these things start. It's not pheromones; it's not astrology! It's statistics!"

"Well, I still don't buy it, Angie." Gwen's jaw was set determinedly.

"And why not?"

"Because," she said defiantly, "that would mean that we

are over the hill." And with that, she lifted her chin, turned on her heel and started walking away. Jessica and Marie each did her own variation of chin lifting and heel turning and followed her. This was not even possible! My friends, my feet-on-the-ground, stable, intelligent, magnificent friends were acting like total ninnies! I had to do something; I had to Intervene! I had to find my voice and say something really brilliant to bring them to their senses.

"You ninnies!" I hollered. I had found my voice, though obviously the brilliant part hadn't caught up yet. "You rat finks!"

The three of them stopped but did not turn around.

"What is the matter with you three? You cowards!" I was starting to gather a crowd. "Are we just supposed to wilt and fade away because we are no longer ingénues? What's the magic age? Are we old, useless hags at forty? Fifty? Because our bodies change and go into the next phase of life?"

"You go, girl!" a little white-haired lady called out.

"And who is it that's telling us we're all used up because we're not twenty or thirty anymore? Madison Avenue? Since when did we ever knuckle under to those mealy-mouthed pollsters and ad agency tyrants? As women in this generation, we've made our own rules!"

I had won the support of the growing crowd, parts of which were getting pretty riled. Women in the crowd raised their liver-spotted fists, elbowing bewildered spouses for punctuation. Too bad we didn't have someplace to march. Even my three friends had turned around to pay attention.

"Gwen, you spent your entire life bursting through doors previously closed to women, battling with men on their own turf. Are you going to throw in the towel because you don't want to admit to a couple of wrinkles and a few hot flashes?"

"Go, Mom!" Jenna's voice came through the crowd. Did I mention that Sacramento is a very, very, *very* small place? I looked up to see Jenna, Ryan, Tyler, and Cyndee strolling down the sidewalk toward me. Their faces, in order, exhibited excitement, bewilderment, bemusement, and horror. Many say that it's a parent's duty to become an embarrassment to their children; I was clearly going above and beyond the call. But I couldn't stop. I was on a roll.

"And you, Marie. Ready to throw away one of the best relationships I've ever seen. Just because you're unwilling to admit that maybe, just maybe, you're not acting rationally because of crazy mood swings caused by menopause. That's right! Menopause! I said the word out loud. That shameful, embarrassing stage of life where we women are supposed to curl up and retreat and die!" Was I foaming at the mouth yet? My adrenaline seemed to be taking a direct route to my mouth, not stopping to check in with my brain.

"And what about you, Jessica? You're one of the most well read, interesting, unique women I know. Since when did Britney Spears become your role model? Since when did chasing men become your only mission? And since when did you prefer guys who think false eyelashes, fake nails, and ridiculous shoes are more important than intelligence and character? One-night stands rather than real relationships?"

"Yeah, get a vibrator," someone in the crowd mumbled.

"We've spent years banging our heads against glass ceilings to prove that women are equal to men and not second-class citizens. We fought battles for sexual equality that our daughters never even knew existed. We have been the warrior maidens, breaking into unknown territory. And now, are we going to let a few gray hairs defeat us after all that? A few raging hormones? We've been through trials by fire; are we not tough enough to brave a few hot flashes? Is that the legacy we want to leave our children?"

"No way!" Jenna and Tyler shouted together. They high-fived each other and grinned. I may be an idiot but I made some pretty terrific children. Were Che Guevera's kids this supportive? I doubt it.

"Angie, don't you think . . ."

"Don't you 'Angie' me, Gwen! I'm marching into this seminar because someday I will be menopausal or peri-menopausal or postmenopausal and I'm going to learn about it with my head held high and my eyes wide-open!"

"Geez, Angie! Ease up, will you? I was just saying that the doors are open and we'd better hurry if we want to get good seats."

"Oh." I waved to the kids and followed my three best friends through the doors.

Ushers passed out fans as we walked into the auditorium and found our seats. The speaker, an elegant, lively woman who had entered her sixties beautifully was just starting her presentation.

"Those of you who have experienced full-blown hot flashes have no doubt about the source of global warming, right?" The audience giggled appreciatively. "But some of you may not even be sure if you've had a hot flash. Maybe you just thought that Sacramento has had an unseasonably warm spring this year."

"Ah-ha!" I stage-whispered to my friends. "See what I mean?"

"Historically, we've associated menopause solely with hot flashes for a couple of reasons. For one, it's a symptom that our male-dominated medical community can't palm off as 'typical female hysteria.' But for another, many of the other symptoms sneak up on us and could be caused by a number of factors. So let me introduce you to a few of these other, less famous symptoms of The Change." She flipped a huge list onto the screen.

"So," she continued, "we have those delightful irrational bouts of anger and rage, often followed by a sense of complete hopelessness." I nodded significantly at Marie; she glared back at me. "Then how about this one? The aggravating inability to concentrate, multitask, or maintain a logical sequence in your thinking." My poke to Gwen's ribs earned me a swat on the arm. "And some of us find that we have a dramatically increased, almost unbearable libido level."

"See?" I hissed at Jessica.

"Angie, knock it off or you can go sit by yourself!" she hissed back.

"I'm just saying that . . ."

"Sshhh!" Half the audience shushed me. Satisfied that I had won my point anyway, I settled back into my seat. My comfortable seat. With the nice armrests and high, padded back. If I slouched down, I could just lean my head back into it. And close my eyes for just a moment. This Active Intervention sure is exhausting work . . .

By the time the speaker had identified sleeplessness as a possible symptom, I was snoring peacefully.

Chapter 17

The next week everything seemed to be—dare I say it?—going very well. I had no definitive proof yet, but first indications were very positive.

#1. *I spotted Jack in the backyard dancing a little fox trot as he watered the plants, humming "It's delightful, it's delicious, it's de-lovely!" He looked chipper enough to leap up and kick his heels together. I'm sure only his lumbago kept him from doing so.*

#2. *Gwen's secretary called to inform me that she had been directed to set up an appointment for me to see Gwen's new naturopath and get my hormonal levels checked. Gwen had also instructed her to send me a list of books about hormone therapies for my edification. The poor young woman sounded exhausted.*

"Is Gwen back in action then?"

"I think so, Mrs. Hawkins. She must have been in here this weekend. Stacks that have been gathering on her desk for over a month are complete and back on my desk for immediate attention."

#3. *Jessica called to ask about a good place to donate clothes.*

"I'm looking at some of the things I've bought recently and just think they are not quite right energetically speaking. Are false eyelashes recyclable?"

#4. *On Wednesday, I heard from Jenna.*

"Mom, I just wanted to call and let you know that Ryan and I are heading off to Bodega Bay for a few days."

"That's sounds very romantic, sweetie. Of course wasn't that the place where Hitchcock filmed *The Birds*? That scary movie where flocks of killer birds swarm into town and Tippi Hedren gets stuck in the bedroom upstairs . . ."

"Mom!"

"Uh, sorry, sweetie."

"We thought it would be good to get out of town and talk this all through. In general though, I'm feeling much better about it. Marriage, I mean."

"You are?"

"Yeah. I guess I was really just afraid of losing myself. That to be married to Ryan, I had to become someone else, more staid, more responsible, more . . . I don't know, boring I guess."

"So what changed?"

"Seeing you on the Community Center steps the other night. You were really something, Mom." I could feel her grinning over the phone. "And I realized that you never became someone that you're not. You are still who you really are."

"True, if you assume that who I really am is a ranting, raving idiot."

"No, Mom." Jenna laughed. "Who you are is someone who stands up for her friends, her family, what she believes, all the important stuff."

"Jenna, I can't promise you that you won't go through some changes being married. Everyone does to some extent."

"I know, Mom, but the essential me, who I really am, needs to remain intact, or maybe evolve and grow. But not hide out. I think I've been hiding out with Ryan. I love Ryan, Mom. And if he really loves me, he'll take me for who I really am, right? And if he doesn't want the real me, better that I find out now, right?"

"Jenna, I just have one piece of advice."

"Yes, Mom?"

"While in Bodega, stay out of upper bedrooms in old farmhouses . . ."

On Thursday night, Tyler picked me up for our date together at the gym.

"Mom," he said as we drove downtown, "do you have some spare room in your storage unit for me to put some stuff for a while? I'm going to crash with Jenna until I can find a new place."

A new place? A Cyndee-less place? It took every card in the deck to keep my face from bursting into a joyful grin at the thought.

"Well, sure, honey. But did something happen between you and Cyndee?"

"Yep. She dumped me."

She what! That two-bit floozy dumped my precious son, the best thing that will ever come into her life? Wait'll I get hold of her! I'll pop those phony boobs so flat they'll . . . "Oh, really, Tyler? I'm so sorry to hear that, honey. Did she happen to say why?" That little twit! I'll send her perky little body parts to the other side of the moon, Alice!

"Actually, Mom"—Tyler turned to me with a grin—"after hearing about your escapade in jail and seeing you in action on the Community Center steps, she started doubting the stability of my gene pool."

Uh-oh. My fault. Again. Why do all calamities turn out to be my fault? "Tyler, I'm so sorry. Maybe if I talk to her . . ."

"No, Mom. Truth is that I've been thinking of calling it off for a while. I just didn't know how. But you did it for me." He grinned again. "Thanks, Mom. I owe you one."

"Sure, honey. Anytime you want me to embarrass myself in public to help you out, just let me know."

"Thanks, Mom." He smiled again. "See, Cyndee is nice and all." Yes, the "and all" part was obvious. "But I guess she wasn't really my type. Honestly, Mom, I don't know what my type is. Maybe I'll never know; maybe I'm just not very good at romance." Tyler looked a little sad and wistful.

"Honey, give it some time. If you worry too much about it, you'll crimp up your garden hose."

"My what?"

"Uh, scratch that last comment, Tyler. I just mean that you have plenty of time, and you are a wonderful man. It'll work out, honey. I just know it."

"Thanks, Mom." We drove to the gym in companionable silence and mutual appreciation.

The Guys must have been forewarned that I was bringing Tyler because they had formed a reception line at the door, looking much like the defensive line of the Oakland Raiders.

"You Angie's kid? You better be good to her. Not like I was to my old lady. You don't be good, and I'm gonna . . ."

"Back off, Bobby. He's a good kid, aren't you kid? Did she tell you that it's okay for a man to cry?" The Guys took Tyler under their beefy wings to the other side of the gym. I spotted Tom and ran over to report.

"Tom! It's working! That hose thing! Everyone seems to be doing better, Jenna sounds more like herself, and Tyler just told me that he broke up with his girlfriend!"

"Ah, then the timing is even better." Tom stepped aside to reveal a beautiful young woman working out with free weights at the mirror. Her shining black hair was pulled back in a long ponytail; deep-set eyes looked intense as she worked bicep curls (her weights were not pink with tassels). "Angeline, come meet Mrs. Hawkins." The lovely young woman smiled over her shoulder, slowly put her weights down, and approached gracefully.

"Mrs. Hawkins, I am so glad to meet you. My grandfather has told me so much about you." Her eyes sparkled with intelligence and amusement.

"Oh, please, just call me Angie. Do people ever call you Angie?"

"No, never." Her smile was warm and wise, the twenty-something, female version of Tom. "But I would be honored to call you Angie. From what my grandfather has told me, you have great heart and great spirit."

"Well, I suppose that's one way to look at it."

"Angeline is in her second year at McGeorge." Tom beamed proudly.

"Really? So you're studying to be a lawyer?"

"Yes, it's been my dream since I can remember," she said, almost shyly.

"What a coincidence." I looked at Tom suspiciously. "Angeline, you really should meet my son . . ."

I knew just the person to call when I got home, just the person who would be dying to hear all of the good news.

"Angie, don't you realize that there is a time difference between California and Georgia? I may be an old woman, but I still sleep sometimes," Lilah said irritably.

"This is worth waking up for, Lilah. Tyler broke up with Cyndee!" I proceeded to tell her everything: Jenna's insights, Tyler's breakup and new connection, the aunties. I chose to leave out the part about my jail experience; it wasn't really material to the story, was it?

"Well, Angie, you did it. I don't know how you did it, but you have always managed to do it, and you've done it again. Congratulations, my dear." Lilah's certainty that I had personally produced all of these results was perhaps misplaced, but I was too happy to correct her. "Do you think you could do something about Bob and that woman?"

"Uh, I'm afraid that one is out of my hands, Lilah."

"Too bad. But I may have some good news of my own. Remember that brooch I gave you right after your wedding? Do you still have it?"

Ugh! That brooch was the ugliest piece of jewelry I have ever laid my eyes on. It was huge and heavy, gold with unidentifiable semiprecious stones in it. I think it was supposed to be some kind of mythical bird rising from the ashes upside down, or maybe it was the Statue of Liberty holding a bouquet of dandelions. Hard to tell, but it was awful. For over twenty years, I had kept that brooch and worn it like a hair shirt every time Lilah came into town. When Bob and I split up, I almost threw it out. But as Lilah always reminds me, Bob might have divorced me, but she never did.

"Sure. I've still got it."

"It really is the ugliest thing ever created, isn't it, my dear?"

"What? You think it's ugly?"

"Of course. I may be an old woman, my dear, but I still have a sense of style. The truth is that I was not particularly pleased at the circumstances under which you and Bob married. I thought you were some hussy trying to snare him by becoming pregnant. Good manners dictated that I give you something for the wedding. So I went out and found the most god-awful piece I could find."

"So you knew I was pregnant?"

"Of course, I knew! You run off to get married and give birth five months later? I may be an old lady, but I can certainly follow a calendar."

"Oh."

"Anyway, when you wore that ugly sucker year after year, every time I came to visit, well, it was just so dear to me. Such a sacrifice; such loyalty. It almost became beautiful to me."

"Really?"

"No, of course not. Something that tacky will never be beautiful. But you get my drift."

"Yes, Lilah. Uh, thank you?"

"Well, maybe now you can really thank me because I found out that the man who created that piece has become something of a cult hero . . ." Lilah continued with a story that included multiple murders, licentious affairs with members of both genders and several classes of animals, and an alligator with an extraordinary appetite. Don't ask; I couldn't follow the whole thing except that it is a story that could only happen in the heat and humidity of the Deep South.

"The result of this delicious drama is that the piece you have is now worth quite a bit of money."

I was still absorbed in pondering the logistics of an alligator eating so much in one day, so it took me a moment to respond. "Quite a bit? Really?"

"Yes, Angie dear. Let's get rid of it before we all die and someone finds out that I bought something so ugly. I'm not sure of the exact figure it will bring, but it certainly should pay for a wedding. Unless, of course, they decide to rent some island in the Bahamas for the ceremony."

We talked a little longer and agreed that I should send the always-ugly, now-infamous, brooch to her for appraisal. Odds were that they would pay more money for its swampy associations in Georgia than in California.

"You know, Angie dear, you've always been my favorite daughter-in-law."

"Lilah, I'm your only daughter-in-law."

"Yes. Well, perhaps the competition has been slim, but you still would have won the title."

"Lilah?"

"Yes, Angie?"

"Thanks. But let me ask you something. You've called yourself an old woman three times tonight. I've never heard you do that before. Is everything okay?" I asked in my most concerned, favorite-daughter-in-law voice.

"That? I guess I have been a little irritable lately. Sometimes I think the only good thing about being over eighty is that I don't have to worry about dying young. But the real problem is that I'm just not getting any lately; lack of sex makes me cranky. Suppose you could work on that next, my dear? A new paramour for me? Just make sure all his equipment is fully functional, Angie. I don't want one of those broken-down old . . ."

One thing didn't seem to be improving: I still had heard nothing from Tim. I concentrated on visualizing my flowing garden hose, but it invariably made me need to pee. I thought about calling him, but what good would that have done? As Jenna said, if he doesn't care about me as I am— crazy, busy, involved with my friends and family—then better to find out now, right? Maybe I should call him and ask him directly. Don't be stupid, Angie! If he wanted to talk to you, he'd call. Wouldn't he?

Actually, I did dial Tim's number a couple of times—not the whole number of course; I didn't want to get caught by caller ID. But I don't know what I would have said anyway:

"Hi, Tim. Nothing's changed much, so I'm still too busy to see you right now. But it's not because I don't want to see you. I do. It's just that I have other priorities . . ." No, not that. How about: "I just can't fit you in right now." Nope, no good. "There are people more important to me . . ." Ack! Not that. Okay, what about: "Tim, if we lived together, this wouldn't be a problem. See, I'm always awake between the hours of 1:00 A.M. and 5:00 A.M. and . . ." No! Even I would hang up on me.

Maybe I should just give up on the whole dating thing for a while. Take a sabbatical. Not that I really needed to make that decision. It's not like anyone was knocking down my door to take me out. Anyway, most of my love life had been as scintillating as back issues of *Field & Stream*, with a few scenes from *Monty Python* thrown in. So really it should come as no surprise that my romantic life was not proceeding exactly as planned or as hoped. Whose does?

Jenna returned from Bodega Bay and bounced through my front door with her old glow and most importantly:

"Your hair! Jenna, that peacock blue has always been my favorite! It's perfect on you!"

"Well, I figured this was the easiest way to handle the

'something blue' part of the wedding. Because, Mom, I'm getting married!"

"Oh, Jenna!" We hugged and spun around the kitchen. We high-fived then started a two-woman, two-beagle conga line: *Jenna's getting marr-ied! Jenna's getting marr-ied!*

When we finally settled down, she told me about her romantic weekend, the heartfelt discussions, the hand-holding on the beach, the tears, the laughter, the dreams for their future. Maybe I would never have real romance in my own life, but it was wonderful to know my little girl would.

"So, Mom, Ryan's parents have the opportunity to go on a field research project in Inner Mongolia."

"Oh, how fascinating!" Everything in my life was going wonderfully and why shouldn't other people's lives be thrilling too? I was happy for the whole world, even these new in-laws I'd not yet met. Let our garden hoses be un-clamped! Let all wonderful things happen to everyone!

"Yes, but this means that they need to leave in three and a half weeks and they won't be back in the U.S. for eighteen months. Now that I'm really sure about getting married, Ryan and I don't want to wait that long. So I'm wondering if we could have the wedding before they leave. Is that possible?"

Oh.

My garden hose had turned into a fire hose pouring down my throat. A wedding in three weeks? Impossible. It takes ten months just to order a wedding dress and get it made. (Which I'm convinced is a total racket. Heck, you can construct a house in six months and complete all infrastructure required for the Olympics in less than a year. You're telling me that it takes them longer to sew over-priced beads on a dress than it took to build Yankee Stadium?) Invitations had to go out, church and reception hall had to be reserved, those little almond doodads had to be counted into net bags with ribbon ties. Three weeks? Impossible!

Jenna looked at me with wistful brown eyes. Spud and Alli must have taught her that look. It was very good. This very same look had accompanied "Mom, my kindergarten class needs you to bake four dozen cookies for the party tomorrow. Can you do it?" and "Mom, Joey just asked me to the junior high dance tonight! Can we hem my new dress by five o'clock?" My answer then was the same as it was now:

"Of course, it's possible, sweetie. We'll just need to . . ."

"Oh, Mom"—Jenna threw her arms around me—"thank you, thank you, thank you! I'm so happy! I'm running over to Ryan's to tell him right now." She flew out the door. "I love you, Mom!"

"I love you too, sweetie," I mumbled to the empty space. When my stunned brain cranked back into gear, I knew just what to do. I e-mailed the Mounties, my posse, my best friends:

Guess what? Jenna is now getting married in THREE weeks! HELP ME! Be here tomorrow morning at 8:00 AM sharp for an emergency meeting. Angie needs saving again!

I put on my jammies and brushed my teeth, the beginning of my nightly ritual that was unlikely to result in

sleep. I picked up my dictionary and started reading where
I'd left off the night before:

Quixotic: 1) extravagantly and romantically inclined; pro-
foundly devoted despite material considerations 2) vi-
sionary, pursuing lofty goals 3) ridiculously impractical,
foolhardy, preposterous . . .

Sancho? Are you out there?

Chapter 18

The last time the team had gathered to plan something was for the Angie Hawkins Crisis Intervention Project. That project had to do with keeping me out of a blackmail scheme that would have ruined my son's life and left me without my favorite black lace thong. Hard to explain; you had to be there.

But if the team could succeed on that previous critical mission, surely we could succeed in planning a simple little wedding. In less than three weeks. With no financial support from the bride's father. Banking on the potential value of a brooch that was uglier than a turkey's wattles. Using a team of women who, as of a week ago, were completely wacko and unreliable thanks to raging hormones. What had I been thinking? I was trusting my daughter's happiness on a hormonally challenged team of the Three Stooges. I took extra deep breaths to quell my panic.

"Yoo-hoo!" Marie called cheerily through my front door.

"Are you ready for us?" She floated gracefully into my studio, with a bouquet of flowers and a bag of muffins. "I thought we should make this meeting a little festive," she trilled as she gently pulled a vase out of my cupboard. Okay, so Marie appeared to be back to her mellow, gracious self. She wore a slightly clingy knit dress and had a morning-after-the-night-before sparkle in her eye, which might explain Jack's Fred Astaire routine. I felt a glimmer of hope.

"Good morning, everyone!" Gwen followed in Marie's footsteps. I looked at her carefully but couldn't tell; she looked energetic, unwrinkled, nearly Gwen-perfect but . . .

"Gwen, could you hold that door open for me?" Jess wrestled her flip chart into my living room/bedroom/office. Jess was wearing—yes!—her pink Birkenstocks and her face had returned to its natural, beautifully unadorned state.

"What's that thing for?" Gwen asked.

"To help plan the wedding."

"Whose wedding?" Gwen's face looked completely blank, several chips short of a full circuit board. Uh-oh. The intellectual powerhouse of the team was still unplugged. It's not that the rest of us aren't smart. We are. But Gwen is (was?) exceptionally brilliant, and I had been banking on exceptional brilliance to get us through this wedding emergency. Without her . . . I started my deep breathing. My three friends burst out laughing.

"Oh, Angie, I was just pulling your leg! Relax, will you? You'll hyperventilate that way!" Gwen's face took on her blessedly familiar patronizing look.

We made ourselves coffee, my three resurrected-from-insanity best friends talking all at once.

"I found the best Web site! It's called *PowerSurge* and it has interviews, tips for symptoms like vaginal dryness . . ."

"My doctor prescribed a low-dose birth control pill. I'm also drinking black cohosh tea which has completely wiped out my hot flashes . . ."

"You have to listen to this CD I brought! It's called *Menopause the Musical,* and it's hysterically funny! The show should be coming to town soon and . . ."

"You've got to try wild yam cream! I rub it on my wrists twice a day, and it's great for . . ."

"Hold it!" I yelled over the enthusiastic twittering. "We're here to plan a wedding, and time is running out!"

"What are you so testy about, Angie? You're the one who got us into this menopause thing in the first place," Marie protested.

"I did not get you into menopause. You were in menopause, and I merely . . ."

"Well, you don't have to be so snippy about it," Gwen said. "Have you made that appointment to have your hormone levels checked?"

"Gwen, I promise I'll do that, but can we please talk about the wedding?"

Jess went to her flip chart, marker in hand. "Okay, so Angie, what have you done so far?"

"Uh, well, nothing really."

"Nothing?" Gwen arched her eyebrow. "What on earth have you been doing this past month?"

Actually, I've been doing a little jail time for you, Gwen,

taking Jess to the ER, letting Marie's husband cry on my shoulder. . . .

"Never mind," Gwen continued, as I sputtered wordlessly. "Let's get started now and try to make up for the time Angie lost."

"Hey, can an old rooster join this hen party?" Jack called from the door. "I brought some fresh-squeezed carrot and spinach juice. The guy at the health food store said it was great for everything from itchy skin to mood swings. He didn't mention receding hairlines." Jack rubbed his mostly bald head with a grin.

"Of course, Jack. You are always welcome with or without . . ."

"Good morning, Mom!" Jenna bounced through the door with Tyler close behind. The kids hugged their favorite aunties and honorary uncle, and we shuffled chairs around to fit us all into my tiny studio. "I told Gran about our meeting, and she asked to join in via phone," Jenna announced as she dialed Lilah's number. "Ryan flew home to help his parents pack so they can come to the wedding. He sends his love."

"I've been up and waiting for hours! What's wrong with you people? Does no one in California have an alarm clock?" Lilah squawked over my speaker phone.

"Good morning, Lilah!" we chanted together.

"Sweetie, did you bring your wedding project binders?"

"No, Mom," Jenna grinned. "You see, I think it's more about the marriage than the wedding. Let's just plan a kick-ass party. We don't need dusty old rules or somebody else's checklists to do that. I've got a team of party animals here who will know just what to do." My real daughter, the Jenna I have loved from birth, was officially and irrevocably back.

"Now this is the kind of wedding I can sink my dentures into!" Lilah yelled.

"Okay." Jess started writing on her flip chart. *"A Kick-Ass Wedding Party.* Let's capture the main issues first, like venue."

"Food, music," Marie offered.

"Guest list, invitations," Gwen added.

The team was on a roll. I started to relax, my eyes heavy from exhaustion. But as we came to the end of the issues list, I came to with a start: "Budget," I croaked. "Sweetie, I'm afraid that I don't know yet how much that brooch will bring and . . ."

"Mom, don't worry about it. Where there's a will there's a way. Let's assume a budget of zero and see how creative we can be."

"She's right, Angie," Marie enthused. "I'm sure we've all got favors we can call in . . ."

"Maybe we could charge admission?" Lilah ventured.

"Or rifle through guests' wallets," Gwen mused.

"Gwen! You can't mean . . ."

"Angie," Jess admonished me sternly, "you know the rules of brainstorming. There are no bad ideas."

And so the Kick-Ass Wedding Party team started brainstorming. Obstacles like lack of time were obliterated.

"We'll send invitations by e-mail."

"What if they don't have e-mail?"

"Who doesn't have e-mail these days?"

"So we could fax to those people who don't have e-mail."

"What if they don't have a fax?"

"Well, surely, everyone has a phone. If they don't have e-mail and they don't have fax, we'll just call them."

Jess would arrange for an 800 number, an automated RSVP center. Tyler and Jack volunteered to build a Web site for Jenna and Ryan's gift wish list.

"Just like Amazon.com, we'll make it so people cross off gifts as they get them," Jack enthused. Marie beamed at him, giving Jack a kiss on the cheek that made him blush.

Marie had dozens of caterers and restaurateurs who owed her favors for referrals in the past. "They've made plenty of money off me, and I'm sure they won't mind. The only expense will be the cost of the food itself, which should be minimal if we plan it right."

"But no cheap wines!" Gwen insisted. "Let's track down some really good wines. I've got some pretty well heeled clients. I'm sure they'll come through for us."

We were stumped for a few minutes when it came to venue. What hall or church could we reserve at such short notice and get for free no less?

"I've got it! I've got the most scathingly brilliant idea!" Jenna clapped her hands. "Let's have it where Ryan proposed to me!"

"In a barn?" I said doubtfully.

"Sure! It's a great farm, outside of Woodland. The couple who own it are very sweet, and Ryan has saved more than one of their animals. I'm sure they would let us. And we could clean it up . . ."

"Woodland. That has a nice ring to it. Very pastoral.

Much better than having to announce that my grand-daughter is getting married in Sacramento . . ."

"The weather should be nice so we could hold it out-doors . . ." Gwen offered.

"And in the country, you'll even be able to see the stars at night. How romantic!" Marie cooed.

"Oooo! And the moon will be quarter full about that time," Jess added. "Very positive astrologically and ener-getically for blossoming love! I can just picture it!"

All I could picture was cow patties and horseflies, but I deferred to the bride and the rest of the team, who were very enthusiastic.

Attire for the wedding party was next on the list.

"Well, the men can just rent tuxes or wear suits. No problem there."

"Maybe with cowboy boots?" Lilah ventured.

"That would be cute, Gran. And very practical. But what about you bridesmaids and matron?"

The four of us looked at one another. To say that we don't subscribe to the same fashion statement is like saying that Newt Gingrich and Ralph Nader differ ever so slightly in their political agendas. Jess, now that she was no longer trolling for boy toys, tended toward diaphanous fairy-queen dresses. Gwen was immaculately and expensively tailored; Marie, no longer playing the old, sexless hag, draped herself in deep exotic colors and sensuous fabrics. Me? Well, let's just say that my clothes were classic, mean-ing that most of them had been in my closet for more than a decade. My clothes had never been in, nor would they ever be out of, style.

"I have an idea," Gwen volunteered. "We don't have time to get dresses made, and we are different body types and styles. Why don't we just agree on a good color for all of us and everyone go out and find her own dress in that color? Would that be okay, Jenna?"

"Sure. That would work great! So what color?"

This, of course, was not going to be an effortless conversation. Gwen weighed in on the "in"- or "out"-ness of specific colors while Jessica factored in their energetic properties and cosmic significance. Marie had strong opinions about complementing hair color and skin tones. All I contributed was my lifelong fear of orange. After much discussion, the group determined that purple, being relatively universal, would be the designated color.

"Okay, so now we need to cover music," Jess read from our list. "Angie, do you think Tim might be able to . . . ?"

"Uh, Tim and I aren't seeing each other anymore."

The team went silent for a few moments.

"Why not, Mom? I thought you really liked him."

"I did. I do. But it just didn't work out."

"You never did the nasty with him, did you? I tell you, Angie, men won't wait for . . ."

"Lilah! It's got nothing to do with that. Look, let's not get off track here. We need to find someone other than Tim to help."

After a long sympathetic pause, Tyler looked at Jenna, and said, "Okay, don't worry about it. I think I know how to get the music covered. Jenna, I'll need your help. What's our next topic?"

"Well, actually, team, we've just got one left. Jenna's dress," Jess announced.

"Short of Cinderella's fairy godmothers flying in, I don't know how we'll get a dress made in time," Gwen observed grimly.

"May I offer a suggestion?" Lilah asked. "Sweet Pea, would you consider wearing my wedding dress? The one I wore for my very first wedding in '42? Of all six of them, it's always been my favorite."

"Oh, Gran, I would love to wear your dress!" Tears rolled down Jenna's cheek; there wasn't a dry eye in the team.

"Of course, I can't even tell you what size it is. I wore it in the days when a size twelve was what they now call a size six. Good heavens, what on earth has the fashion industry been thinking? Why, I practically have to buy size zero these days and there are women smaller than me. What are they? Size minus four . . . ?"

And the Kick-Ass Wedding Party was planned.

In bed that night, I once again lay awake and studied the ceiling. Not that there was really a lot to study on my ceiling. It wasn't like calculus or anything. But there was a spider's web in the far corner that had started about a month ago. It was getting pretty interesting . . .

That discussion about music for the wedding had me thinking about Tim again. Not that I needed any prompting. In fact, it was only with great effort that I didn't think about him. What if Tim was the last good man to come along? What if nobody else's smile ever made me feel the way that Tim's smile did? What if . . . ? I looked at Spud and Alli snuggled beside me. I figured it could be worse. I could have fallen for a guy who snored as loudly as Alli and was as hairy as Spud.

Fallen? Did I say fallen?

"Well, guys. Looks like it's just you and me from here on out."

Chapter 19

The next few weeks flew by in a well-organized flurry of activity. Now that we were all back to normal (normal still being a relative term) the whole team performed like a well-trained circus troupe. There were wires walked, flames swallowed, flying bodies caught in midair, lions tamed—all with well-ordered precision. (Fortunately, we weren't required to wear those skintight spandex jumpsuits for this performance. My cellulite would never forgive me for squashing it into one of those things.)

Jess, in charge of the twenty-four-hour automated RSVP hot line, reported that attendance would be healthy. Jenna had trashed the notion of ranking her guests along with the wedding planning binders. So Jess, Jenna, and I held a conference regarding seating arrangements:

"But we have to do some kind of seating chart. Otherwise, Uncle Gus might sit next to someone in Ryan's family. Three minutes of listening to Gus, sweetie, and they'll demand an annulment."

"Well, how about alphabetically, Mom?"

"Lilah next to the Martin cousins from New Jersey? We'd have to bring in UN Peacekeeping troops to avoid bloodshed."

"Obviously, the best way to handle this," Jess advised, "is to seat people by astrological sign. You wouldn't want a Leo with a Taurus, for instance, or a Gemini with a Virgo. However, if you concentrate on the twelfth house and . . ." After fifteen minutes of Jessica's totally incomprehensible dissertation of houses, and moons, and houses with moons in the door, Jenna and I left seating in her very capable, if somewhat eccentric, hands.

Jack and Tyler spent a couple of all-nighters getting the Web site up and running. It was magnificent, with Jenna and Ryan's wish list and links to sites where the products could be purchased. Many of the requested gifts were from *PetVet on the Net;* Tyler and Jack added definitions of certain items, wisely determining that some of them (e.g. sphygmomanometers) required explanation.

"Mom, did you know that Jenna requested this thing that pokes up into a horse's . . ."

"Yes, honey, I know. And those are probably very difficult to wrap. Let's recommend a gift certificate option for the squeamish."

Lilah's wedding dress arrived via overnight delivery. As predicted, Lilah's size twelve had morphed into a size six over the years. To fit Jenna's size four, which had more bust and less hip than her grandmother, it needed to be altered. This was Gwen's assignment.

"Mom! You should have seen Auntie Gwen! She was magnificent!"

"Really, sweetie? What happened?"

"We walked into the alterations shop and she threw six St. John's suits on the floor!" That's easily seventy-five hundred dollars' worth of dramatic entrance. "Then she stood nose to nose with the owner of the shop, and said 'These need to be altered. But these mean nothing to me! They are rags. Throw them out!' The alterations lady was stunned. Then Auntie Gwen said, 'Because if my god-daughter cannot have her wedding dress altered in time for her wedding date by the best seamstress in California, then I care not what I wear!' "

"So let me guess, sweetie. The alterations lady swore to have your dress done in time or die in the effort?"

"Yeah. It was amazing. Is Auntie Gwen really my god-mother?"

"Not exactly, sweetie. But if you ever need a really good trial lawyer . . ."

The three bridesmaids and I tried on every purple dress within a three-county region. Geez! Who knew there were so many shades of purple? The purple compatibility issue was becoming critical. After the first week of our dress reconnaissance, Marie, having ordained herself Commander in Chief of Color, called an emergency meeting.

"Okay," Marie began, sounding very much like General Patton, "I think we're spinning our wheels on this mission, and we don't have time to be inefficient. So I've come up with a purple standardization methodology that should keep us on track." She pulled out several huge boxes of Crayolas. "We need to distinguish the good purples from the bad and go from there."

After a lively discussion and vigorous coloring, both inside and outside the lines, it was determined that the bad purples included Red Violet, Eggplant, Wisteria, and a color inexplicably named Jazzberry Jam. Our good purples included, but were not limited to, Royal Purple, Purple Mountain Majesty, Violet Purple, and Purple Heart.

"All right, troops," Marie ordered, "let's roll." Armed with our crayons, we marched back out to the battlefields of retail fashion once again, keeping in tight communication via four-way calling:

"Okay, I've got a Purple Heart and a Royal Purple to choose from," Marie announced. "How about the rest of you?"

"I found the most elegant Purple Mountain Majesty, and the store is trying to get it in my size. Other than that, I'll have to go with the Blue Violet," Gwen offered.

"Heck, I thought I had a Violet Purple but when I got it in the light it was really Wisteria. But I have a Purple Heart backup," I added.

"My Vivid Violet looks good but the Blue Violet won't have to be hemmed," Jess concluded.

"Okay," Marie summed up. "It sounds as if we've got a Royal Purple, a Blue Violet, a Purple Heart, and a Vivid Violet. How do they look?" We all pulled out our Crayolas and colored furiously.

"Gwen, I really think we need you in Purple Mountain Majesty," Jess voted.

"Okay. I'll call the store's headquarters in New York."

*   *   *

Food and catering was also Marie's bailiwick.

"Angie, meet me at Mace's at eleven o'clock. Show up and shut up. Leave all the talking to me."

Before entering the restaurant, Marie coached me to look stern and mysterious, like Jimmy Hoffa. Lacking Hoffa's definitive hairline and smarmy smile, I chose my poker face instead: two of hearts, three of diamonds . . . We were escorted through the restaurant and sat across an unset table from the restaurant owner, Bruce Mace.

"My client," Marie started, mumbling in a raspy Marlon Brando voice, "has a wedding. An important wedding. A family wedding." Per instruction, I stared at the saltshaker and tried not to giggle. "And for this important family wedding, she needs a favor. Do I make myself clear?"

"Sure, Marie. But what's wrong with your voice? You want help with a wedding? I'd be happy to help."

"My client would not take it kindly if you do not take this favor seriously. She has many important friends, if you know what I mean, who . . ." Talk about method acting! Marie eyes had a sinister gleam in them and she cocked her head to one side, nodding like Don Corleone.

"Heck, Marie, you've always been good to us. I'm really happy to help out however I can . . ."

"My client never asks for a second favor once the first favor has been refused. But this would be a great service to the family . . ."

"Marie! For gosh sakes, he said yes. Give it a rest, will you?"

"Oh." Marie snapped to, shaking her head and clearing her throat. "Thanks, Bruce. That's awfully nice of you."

219

* * *

The wine operation was critical. If you live in California the expectation—no, the requirement—is that you serve only excellent wines at every function. You can skimp on wine for events like potluck dinners (especially if you won't be identified as the one who brought the second-rate bottle) but generally your entire reputation is based on how well you pick your wines. Is this fair? Of course not. Just because we're from California doesn't mean we can determine whether a wine is multifaceted, medium-bodied, or simply mediocre. Does everyone in Detroit understand the nuances of power-train assembly? Oh. They do? Who knew?

Fortunately, Gwen led the charge on our critical wine mission. After several days of clandestine meetings and secret negotiations, she called us together one evening for the tasting. The drapes of her living room were pulled shut, and she asked to arrive three minutes apart and park a block away.

"Okay," she said, when we had all gathered. "We need to choose between these wines. But you must all promise not to breathe a word to anyone about our final decision."

"I don't get it, Gwen. What's the big secret?" Jessica inquired innocently.

"I've got two clients vying for the honor of supplying wines for Jenna's wedding," Gwen revealed with a smile. "And I can't alienate the loser."

"Ah!" we all said knowingly.

"So they are both willing to supply wine for the entire wedding?" Jenna asked incredulously.

"It's a matter of enological honor, a serious affair in California," Gwen replied solemnly. "In fact, at this point, I'll have to accept wines from both of them to avoid the issue ending up in a duel."

"Ah!" we all said knowingly again.

"But whatever will you do with all the wines we don't use for the wedding?" Marie continued.

"I'll just have to find some friends to drink it with me over the next several months," Gwen replied gravely.

"Ah!" we all said happily.

Finally, we proceeded to some serious tasting. The rest of the team categorized our wine candidates as "oaky," "fruity," "earthy," etc. My own categories were more basic: "icky" or "yummy." (After several rounds of tastes, most of my sips fell into the "yummy" group.) By the time Jack arrived to be our designated driver home, the wedding wines were chosen.

By the night of the rehearsal dinner, our wedding project, aka Kick-Ass Wedding Party, was in pretty good shape.

What's the deal with wedding rehearsals anyway? The person who has been in a thousand weddings (minister/ official) doesn't really need to rehearse. Everyone else involved is much too excited or nervous or emotionally wrought to pay attention. So the rehearsal never looks like the real thing. I'll bet Bob Fosse would run a wedding rehearsal to be more like the actual performance:

"Okay, Minister, you're on. Let's see that beatific smile. That's the one. You're better than us, and you know it. Sell it, baby! Very good. Fiddle with your glasses. That's it.

"Okay, Groom. Yes, that's you. Stand up by the minister. Look pale, like you're going to pass out. That's it. Good. Now you can either grin like a loon or shake like a Jell-O mold in a crosswind. You like the Jell-O option? Okay, so shake. That's it. But you can add in the loony grin at any time.

"Minister, if you want to add some drama now, just clear your throat and look sternly at the groom. Yes! Very nice effect! Now you're shaking, baby!

"Okay, Groom, now turn to your best man—yeah, that guy smirking behind you—and whisper 'Are you sure you got the ring?' Good. Just like that. With panic in your voice. Yes, panic. Good.

"Best Man, you whisper back, 'Hey, don't sweat it.' Then dig in your pocket to check. Okay. I want you two to repeat this routine every seven seconds. Got it? Every seven seconds.

"Okay, Bridesmaids, you're up next. I want you to sashay up the aisle like you own the place. It's not like you're going to get lost on the way, right? Now start out in time to the music. Good, but now your escort has no sense of rhythm, and throws you off-balance. Yes, that's it. Now take charge and try to get the poor klutz back on track. That's it. Good. Stomp on his toes if you need to, ladies. That's it; show him who's boss. Okay, now when you get to the platform, jostle each other and make 'psst' noises until you're in formation. Good. Use your elbows if you have to, ladies. Now tuck in each other's bra straps. Very nice.

"Okay, Bride, your turn. Guide your father down the aisle. No, he can't see because he's blubbering. In fact, you may need to carry him partway. And remember, you're in a dress that weighs more than you do. That's it. Drag it, baby, drag it! Good girl. Now smile, baby. No, not like that. You'll be terrified, and your lips will stick to your teeth. That's it, more like a grimace.

"Best Man, are you still checking for that ring? Every seven seconds until it's on her finger.

"Yes, now, Bride, hand that bouquet to the matron so she fumbles it. That's it, baby. Just out of her reach. Very good . . ."

Our rehearsal, less realistic than the Bob Fosse version, was held at the farm. Tents, complete with modular wooden dance floors, were already set up in the meadow in the back, and the bridal bower was in the front yard. We processed ourselves from the bower to the meadow with great dignity and hardly anyone tripped (me being the hardly anyone). The aunties looked young and excited next to their sincere and solemn escorts. I walked alone and, following Jessica's backside carefully, managing to stay within the aisle and make it to my station. Tyler, replacing the father who was not allowed to attend per Clarisse, walked Jenna down the aisle with tears in his eyes. Jenna giggled and glowed as I've never quite seen her before. Ryan, standing at the altar, looked awestruck; his parents in the seats below looked thrilled and happy.

After the brief practice, which had been interrupted only once by some particularly loud sniffling coming from the Matron of Honor/Mother of the Bride, we sat down to eat our informal dinner. Tables were set outside to take advantage of the beautiful spring sunset.

Ryan's dad rose for the first toast:

"On behalf of my wife and myself, I just want to tell you how thrilled we are that our son has found such a lovely bride with such a wonderful family . . ."

"Aaaaw!" A painful animal-like wail came from Jenna as she leaped up from the table and ran sobbing toward the barn.

"Uh, just hold that thought, will you? Everyone start eating. We'll be back in just a sec." I motioned poor startled Ryan to remain seated and scampered after my daughter.

I ran into the barn and could hear Jenna's muffled sobbing. Where the heck was she? This particular barn was not terribly large, and it was prepped for the wedding so it was swept, uncluttered, and four-legged-animal-free. I looked in stalls, behind racks, and finally isolated the sound to somewhere above me. Uh-oh. The hayloft.

Let me just be clear here and now that I am terrified of heights. Not heights themselves per se. I mean I can view pictures of Everest or look at the Empire State Building and really have no reaction at all. Specifically, the panic only sets in when my personal body is required to be at those heights or actually any height higher than my two-tiered step stool.

And actually, I can keep my panic at a minimum if I am taken up to the aforementioned heights in some form of enclosed carrier with the assistance of something eighty proof or higher. An elevator (not glass enclosed, please) or an airplane (aisle seat, thank you, and I'll have that gin and tonic now if you don't mind) are just fine. But the real, im-mobilizing panic sets in when my own personal body is required to launch my own personal body up or down any particular height.

So if barns came equipped with elevators and built-in bars, I would have had no issue. As it was, staring at an extremely rickety-looking ladder (do they intentionally make ladders that way?), my knees started shaking, and my palms were wet enough to water my houseplants. I could still hear Jenna sobbing; my baby girl needed me! So I touched the first rung.

"Okay, body, let's roll." My body did not move. "This is important, and we need to get to Jenna." My body did not respond. "This is ridiculous! Don't make me argue with you! We're going." No response.

Sometimes when I need to trick my body into doing what's good for it, like exercising or eating leafy green vegetables, I'll do something to boost my courage and distract myself from the odious task at hand. So I started to sing. Because my brain had left the premises as soon as the ladder came into view, I could only think of one song, perhaps inspired by my surroundings:

"Old Mac Donald had a farm. Eee I ee I oh!"

My hands and feet started to move.

"And on this farm he had a cow. Eee I ee I oh!"

I was gaining on it; one foot stepped on the first rung.

"With a moo-moo here and a moo-moo there . . ."

Old Mac Donald had pigs, sheep, and a duck by the time I reached the top. My body might have been distracted, but it had not been quick or enthusiastic on this climb. I clambered through the opening onto the solid floor of the loft. 'Solid' is of course a relative term; Mother Earth, preferably sea level or below, is the only solid surface I've ever believed in. This hayloft floor, with enough space between the planks to allow a clear view of the barn below, did not even register on my scale of solid. I couldn't bring myself to stand, so I scooted a few inches forward on my rear end.

"Jenna?"

She had stopped sobbing and was in the sniffle stage of a breakdown.

"Sweetie? It's Mom. Where are you?"

Jenna's blue-topped, red-cheeked face peered around the corner of a haystack.

"Oh, Mom!" she wailed, and collapsed in a heap.

Damn! "With a cluck cluck here and a cluck cluck there . . ." I scooted forward bun width by bun width across the splintery hayloft until I could pull her into my arms. "Sweetie, what's wrong?"

"Oh, Mom! It's Dad!"

Double damn! With the frantic pace of the last few weeks, I'd completely overlooked that my princess would, of course, be missing her first love, her daddy.

"Mom, I always dreamed of Daddy walking me down the aisle. It's just not fair! Doesn't he love me? Doesn't he care that I'm getting married?"

"Sweetie, of course he cares. It's just that, uh, that . . ." That he's a cowardly, self-centered, henpecked imbecile. "Sweetie, he's just in an awkward situation with Clarisse and all."

"Mom, will you please go and talk to him? You can fix it, I know you can. He'll listen to you. Please, Mommy! Please, please, please!" Jenna hadn't called me mommy since she was three. She turned those beagle eyes on me again.

"Jenna, I'll try, but . . ."

"Oh, thank you, thank you, thank you, Mom!" She crushed me in a hug. "Now let's get back. Gosh, everyone must be worried about us, and we still have all the toasts to do! Mommy, I'm so happy! I just knew you could fix it!"

"Just one problem, Jenna."

"What, Mom?"

"I was very motivated to get up here, sweetie, but now that I'm in my right mind, I doubt I can climb down."

Jenna's eyes widened with recognition. "Oh, my gosh! I'm sorry, Mom. I forgot that you . . ."

"That's all right, sweetie. Just tell Auntie Jessica. She'll know just what to do."

Jessica's skills included, among other things, mountain climbing and the use of herbs to enter altered states. I hoped she would either use the former to get me down or the latter to take me to a permanent altered state, maybe Wisconsin. This would not be the first time that Jessica had helped get me down from someplace that I never should have been up in the first place. Yes, Jess would know just what to do. And as I sat waiting for the Jessica McIntyre Mountain Rescue Team to get me down, I wondered just what the heck I was going to do about Bob.

Chapter 20

I drove over to Bob's house (technically, Clarisse's house) right after the rehearsal dinner. Like Frodo heading off to Mordor with the mystic ring, I felt singularly ill equipped for the mission. What kinds of Orcs and goblins would I encounter? Would Mount Doom (in the person of Clarisse) erupt in a volcanic explosion that would destroy the . . . ? Uh-oh. Looked like I was moving into Grade Seven prehallucination status. Geez, I really needed to get some sleep!

I walked up to the door of the house where Clarisse and the father of my children live. The last time I had been to this house was almost two years before, for a Neighborhood Watch meeting. As I recall the topic that evening was the recent rash of mail disappearances from mailboxes. It never occurred to me that the frequent disappearances of Clarisse and Bob into her kitchen that night signaled the end of my twenty-six years of marriage.

I rang the bell reluctantly, and Bob opened the door immediately as if expecting me.

"Angie, what are you doing here?"

"It's Jenna's wedding tomorrow, Bob, and I need to talk to you."

"Okay. Why don't you come inside?"

"No, uh, let's just sit out here if it's okay with you."

"Clarisse isn't here, Angie, if that's what you're afraid of . . ."

"I'm not afraid, Bob, I just need some fresh air." Actually, the air was pretty damp and cool, and spring mosquitoes (who find me extremely tasty) were rampant. But I'd rather have my blood sucked than enter that house again, especially since my mission was to grovel. Bob and I settled on the porch step, a proper two yards between us like all painfully amicable divorced couples.

"Bob, Jenna is heartbroken because you won't be there to walk her down the aisle."

"I figured you didn't need me at all for this thing."

"What do you mean? You're her father, of course she needs you."

"Not really, Angie. You're the one the kids always go to. You're the one who always made things happen and put events together. You were always so capable in everything, so together. You never needed my participation. I was just the bystander in our family all those years."

The conversation sounded very familiar, and I knew I was about to be blamed for the mess, past and present. Was it really my fault? Was my competence that overbearing? Was I so domineering that I had closed Bob out? For the speckle of truth that was there, there was a pound of something unsaid, some piece of the puzzle missing.

"Bob, I don't think the kids see you that way at all, as

just a bystander. But, honestly, you did seem to back off from them when they became teenagers."

"I suppose that's true. I gave up on a lot of things around then. See, I finally realized I would never be a guest on the Johnny Carson show."

Had that been one of his lifelong dreams? One of his cherished goals? If so, maybe he should have taken up juggling or bought a dog who could count or . . .

"Bob, you know I don't watch TV, but hasn't he been off the air for quite a while now? If that's what you want, shouldn't you try for Jay Leno? Or Oprah? Or how about that cooking show . . . ?"

"Geez, Angie! It's a metaphor, for God's sake! The point is that I realized back then that I was all that I would ever be. I would never be exceptional or do anything extraordinary. I'd hit my pinnacle, and it wasn't all that great."

Bob had given up on life even before he hit forty? Wow. I felt more than a little sad. In his twenties, Bob had been energetic and eager, full of possibility. Now that I thought about it, though, he had withdrawn around that time. He no longer talked about his dreams. TV and a Saturday night six-pack became his main passions. Those were the years when I was holding down a full-time job, and the kids were growing and active, stimulating and demanding. I suppose I wasn't *there* enough for Bob, but it wasn't out of spite. It was out of exhaustion.

"You know what's great about being with Clarisse, Angie? She makes me feel like I'm special, like she needs me, like I'm the best thing that ever happened to her. I never felt that way with you."

Ouch! That hurt! But in truth? Bob never felt that way with me because I had never felt that way about him. He had never been my Prince Charming or the Man of My Dreams or even *My Favorite Martian.* How very sad. And finally, here it was, my missing link, the answer to "What's Clarisse got that I ain't got?"

"So maybe I wasn't as involved with the kids as I could have been, Angie. But you certainly didn't seem to need me or want me around. I'm just trying to clear the air here."

The air had become as clear as a KISS concert with an overactive fog machine running. Images of our twenty-six years together merged into a confusing collage of happy, angry, sad, mundane, thrilling moments. It was hard to believe I had shared all of those moments with the slightly paunchy, balding man before me. But in a sense, I guess I hadn't really shared it with him, had I?

"So, Angie, is there anything you want to say to me? I mean, to clear the air on your side?"

Boy, was there! I felt the delicious fire of a good rant and rave welling up in my solar plexus. What about the time he . . . ? But just before my self-righteous rant erupted, I saw Jenna's sad face pining to have her dad beside her on her wedding day. And I saw a picture of Bob (after the doctor had revived him from his fainting spell), holding the newborn baby Jenna in his arms for the first time. His look had been one of pure awe and pride, a touching moment that was interrupted when she peed all over him. But it was nice while it lasted.

"No, Bob. I just want to tell you that you have been a

good dad. And I'll always be grateful that we married and had the life we did." And that was the truth. I didn't need to add that I was also extremely grateful that he'd left me and that I was happier than I'd been in many years. Why wreck a good sweet ending? I gave Bob a hug.

"Thanks, Angie. I appreciate that. So I'll try to clear it with Clarisse for tomorrow and . . ." Car lights shining on the porch cut Bob off midsentence. The aforementioned Clarisse was home.

She heaved her considerable flank out of the front seat and stomped toward us. I suppose seeing your sweetie on your own front porch in an intimate tête-à-tête with his ex-wife is not the perfect ending to a perfect day. Bob leaped up nervously. I sat perfectly still, hoping to blend into the shadows. What could she do? Sit on me? Geez, I'd be flatter than a . . .

"Uh, Dumpling, Angie just came by to talk about the wedding tomorrow."

Dumpling? He calls her "Dumpling"? Five of diamonds, two aces and a . . .

"Pooky, could you leave us girls together for a few moments?"

"Pooky?" If I ever had a poker face, it was not going to be strong enough to see me through "Dumpling" and "Pooky." However, as Bob exited hastily to the safety of the house, I realized that I was probably about to die at the hands of 234 pounds of insanely jealous womanhood. A polite countenance was the least of my worries.

"Angie, we need to talk."

Right. Talk, and maybe I can sidle off this porch to safety.

I'll just slip the magic ring on my finger to make me invisible and . . .

"Bob has been very upset about this wedding rift. So upset that he has been unable to 'perform' if you know what I mean."

Was she really saying this to me? "Perform?" I don't fancy myself as an expert on ex-wife to other woman etiquette. But I've got to believe that sharing tales about the ex-husband's/lover's performance issues are not encouraged.

"Oh, gosh, well I'm sorry about that, Clarisse . . ."

"Look, Angie, between us girls, I know this is difficult for you. Losing your man and all. But, honestly, I just want to be your friend. You and your girlfriends seem to have so much fun together. I'd like to be part of that. Can't we be girlfriends?"

Huh? She wants to be my buddy? Was this a Grade Eight interactive, holographic hallucination?

Okay, maybe it was time to let bygones be bygones. (What the heck does that mean anyway? Isn't a bygone gone by definition? So what would we really have to "let" anyway?) On the one hand, this woman intentionally stole my husband. On the other hand, he was a husband that (after a lot of postdivorce contemplation) I realized I didn't want. Then again, she didn't know that I didn't want him when she stole him. But even so, she had done me a big favor. But on the other hand, she had really hurt my daughter and was ruining her wedding. Still, figuring out how to be friends with Clarisse would show a real maturity. It could be a true character-building experience. Certainly it would further my personal growth and maybe even qualify me for sainthood.

Nah.

"No, Clarisse. No, we can't. We can't be friends. I don't like you." Clarisse looked shocked, then mean and angry. I continued quickly, my life flashing before me (this time I got beyond the junior high make-out session with Robbie Schumacher and got to senior prom night when Roger Mall and I . . .). "But what we can do is work on being cordial and polite to one another. We can stop power-tripping with one another and be civil. We can do all this because if we really care about Bob and Jenna and Tyler, they deserve it."

Clarisse huffed a little. Had I gone too far? Had I just undone all of my very good groveling with Bob?

"I think she's right, Clarisse." Neither of us had noticed Bob still standing at the screen door. "Let's make peace and go to the wedding." His voice had just a hint of the young Bob's confidence and command presence in it; his posture, if you overlooked the protruding belly, was almost swashbuckling. Clarisse looked surprised, then (God help me!) amorous.

"We'd be happy to be at the wedding, Angie," she said with a seductive wink to the screen door. "And now if you'll excuse us . . ."

I got home that evening feeling relaxed and, well, proud of myself. Bob would be at the wedding, Clarisse and I had a truce of sorts, and I had accomplished all of this by . . . what exactly? Obviously, I hadn't said or done anything particularly brilliant. I had just shown up with my inoperative brain, overactive imagination, unwarranted fears, and low expectations. But I did show up. And maybe if I just kept showing up, life would work out okay.

I brushed my teeth, slipped my jammies on, and, most incredibly (given that tomorrow was the big wedding day), fell instantly and soundly asleep.

Chapter 21

Everything was in place for the wedding. I had checked and double-checked, confirmed and re-confirmed all of the arrangements. Which was clearly unnecessary because the aunties were checking everything as well, and they are frighteningly efficient when their hormones are on track. The only thing we couldn't confirm was the weather, but the weather lady predicted sunny and warm. Which of course meant nothing as the weather lady is invariably wrong.

What is it with these weather people? They must have some part of their brains removed, the part that makes you feel self-conscious when you are consistently wrong about something. Every day weather people all over the world cheerfully, with sincerity and lots of scientific mumbo jumbo mispredict the weather. And the very next morning they get up and do the very same thing with the exact same perky self-confidence they had the day before. Maybe it's like baseball. Maybe in the weather world, if you hit it right even 30 percent of the time, you're considered an all-star. All I hoped was that Sunday would be one of our weather lady's infrequent hits.

Gwen, Marie, and Jessica were all at the farm before I got there, bossing everyone around. Bless my friends!

"Angie, you're late. Your assignment is to check for any remaining cow patties in the meadow where the wedding procession will be. Here's a pitchfork, a shovel, and a bucket. Go to it." Gwen handed me the implements, assuming inaccurately that I would know what to do with them. She hustled toward the reception area to browbeat the caterers. A pitchfork, a shovel, and a bucket? How exactly do these three things come together to gather cow patties? Oh, well, I'd figure it out. I was too excited to do much thinking; spearing a few cow patties might be relaxing. I was just grateful for a physical, nonintellectual assignment.

The next hour or so was consumed in my new duty. I had just figured out that the fresher cow patties really should be scooped, not stabbed, when a voice at my ear startled me.

"Come here often?" I looked up from my cow patties to see Tim with his wonderful hundred-watt smile standing beside me. "I hope you don't mind my being here," he said uncertainly, hopefully. "Tyler and Jenna came to see me. They invited me and asked me to bring the music."

"No, I don't mind. In fact, I'm glad you're here. Really glad. I, uh, missed you."

"Yeah? I missed you, too. Angie, I'm sorry that I was so, um . . ."

"Selfish? Insensitive? Boorish?" I offered.

"Can we settle for 'unaware' and leave it at that?"

"Yes, Tim. And I'm sorry, too. Lately, my life has just been a bit . . ."

"Out of control? Insane? Bizarre?"

"Let's just say 'active.' "

"Angie, that's what I like about you. You have a totally full life without me. But then again, that's what is difficult for me, too. You don't seem to really need me around."

Uh-oh. Déjà vu. Hadn't Bob said the same thing to me just last night? Am I supposed to feign a neediness I don't feel to keep a guy happy? I really didn't want to lose this particular guy. But I really didn't want to lose me in the process either.

"Tim, would 'wanting' you do for now? Because I do want you. Around, I mean, I want you around." I blushed to my very toenails.

" 'Want'? That sounds good." Tim's smile positively glittered. "Look, Angie, I know you want to keep your options open. Do you think I could still be one of those options?"

It was definitely the time for appropriate Active Intervention: I moved within kissing distance. "Yep. Actually, I think you're my very favorite option." The sweet kiss we shared next would have been ever so much more romantic had I not stepped squarely in a fresh cow patty during it. Oh, well, you got to give a guy extra credit for kissing you a second time even though you smell of Eau de Manure.

"All right you two. Knock it off," Jessica yelled from the porch of the farmhouse. "Music Man, get those speakers set up. Angie, get in here so we can get you looking presentable." Tim and I saluted and headed off as ordered.

The owners of the house had turned it over to us for the day, and the upstairs had been transformed into a beauty parlor. Garrauch, Jenna's (and my newly adopted) hairdresser was waiting impatiently.

"Interesting scent, madam." He scrunched his Gallic nose into a look of the purest disdain. The French are particularly good at that look. "You will perhaps wish to shower before we begin."

Garrauch, though often a bit dramatic, was a wonderful hairstylist. He had started doing my hair a few months ago and claimed that he was personally responsible for saving me from a frumpy future. I had asked him just last month when it would be appropriate for me to let my gray hairs show. Putting his hand over his heart, he had announced in stentorian tones:

"When they have shoveled the dirt over my casket completely, madam." I had laughed; Garrauch had not.

We spent the afternoon in a flurry of giggles and nail polish and hair spray and eye shadow. We sounded like one of Jenna's sixth-grade slumber parties, laughing and shrieking at pitches that would strain a soprano, until Garrauch was forced to place cotton in his ears.

"Okay, okay, okay," breathed Jess, wiping her eyes from the last few minutes of girlish glee. "Do we have everything? You know, 'something old . . .' "

"Something new, something borrowed . . ." Marie intoned.

"Something blue," Gwen finished. "Well, the something blue is obvious."

"Something new would be my new undies from Victoria's Secret. Thank you, aunties!" The fairy godmothers had treated Jenna to an X-rated afternoon at Victoria's Secret.

"So that leaves something borrowed and something old. Doesn't Lilah's dress qualify for both of those?" Marie asked.

"Technically, I think they have to be two different items," Gwen, our attorney, weighed in.

The five of us were silent.

"Then," Jenna looked stunned, "we don't have everything we need? I can't get married?"

"Easy, sweetie," I said. "Give us a moment. We've gotten out of worse jams than this."

"It has to be something she carries down the aisle," Marie noted.

"And," Jess continued, "it could either be something old or something borrowed because Lilah's dress could fulfill either of those requirements."

"She borrowed my deodorant. Does that count?" Marie asked.

"I don't think something under her armpits . . ."

"She could carry Spud down the aisle. He's old," I offered.

"Angie, Jenna is not going to carry a beagle . . ."

"I've got it!" Jenna shrieked. "Mom, where's the brooch?"

"It's in my purse to give to Lilah. But, sweetie, you can't mean to . . ."

"Mom, it symbolizes everything! Your marriage to Dad, love for Grandma, sacrifice for the family. It's like full circle

240

and . . ." Jenna was stunned into silence when she unwrapped the tissue paper to reveal the infamous brooch. "Oh. Wow. I hadn't remembered that it was quite so ugly . . ."

"Oh, how awful! Someone made that on purpose? Worse, someone bought that on purpose?" Marie asked.

"Mom, you were very brave to wear this thing all those years."

"It is hideous, isn't it? Energetically, the symbolism would be great," Jess said doubtfully. "But I wonder if something that ugly could negate the positive vibrations . . ."

"But, strictly speaking, I don't think it needs to show," Gwen ruled.

Ah-ha! We spent the next fifteen minutes looking for the perfect hiding place for the ugliest brooch ever made, a place where it wouldn't poke Jenna, rip her dress, or have any chance of being seen. Finally, we looped a long gold necklace through it so that it fell into Jenna's bodice.

"Actually, that tiny bit of tail that still shows is almost intriguing," Gwen opined.

"Sweetie, if your grandmother finds out that we've brought that thing out in public again, she'd feed me to that alligator. Do not let it see the light of day."

"Don't worry, Mom."

The ceremony was to begin at sunset and the sun was lowering in the sky. Wedding guests started arriving as Garrauch put the final touches on Jenna's makeup. The four of us were all ready to go. Admonished by Garrauch to stay standing so we wouldn't become wrinkled, we gathered at the window to watch the wedding guests assemble in the tents in the meadow.

"Will you look at that? There's Clarisse, and she's wearing purple! Who gave her permission to wear our purple?" Jessica said indignantly.

"She looks like Barney with a water retention problem," Marie observed.

"Now stop it! I promised Clarisse that we would all be nice to her. We need to start thinking positive thoughts about her and saying nice things about her."

"Like what exactly?" Gwen demanded.

"Like, um . . . well, like . . ." As many things in life, this was going to be easier in theory than in practice. I was stumped. "Okay, well at least we have to avoid saying or doing anything rude."

"What exactly do you mean by 'rude,' Angie?" Jess asked innocently.

"Oh, you know. Like tripping her so she falls in the duck pond, seating her near that wasp's nest by the side of the house, leading her into a cow patty . . ."

"Hmmmm," Jess responded thoughtfully.

"Look! Lilah's in purple, too. Doesn't she look cute?" Standing near Clarisse, Lilah looked like a tiny grape attached to a huge purple Goodyear blimp.

"Time, everyone!" Garrauch clapped his hands authoritatively. "Downstairs, *vite! Vite!*" He herded us down the stairs and out the back door to wait for our cues. Bob had arrived and stood next to Tyler, looking nervous and proud.

"You look nice, Bob," I said, straightening the tie that snuggled a little too tightly around his neck.

"Angie, this is great! Look at Jenna. Can you believe she is so grown-up and so beautiful? I haven't felt this way since I first saw her in the hospital . . ."

"You're not going to pass out, are you, Bob?"

"No, not like that. Like looking at her, I feel that maybe I've done something really good in my life. Something I can be proud of." Bob smiled with tears in his eyes, which, of course, set my own tears flowing. "Thanks for asking me to be here, Angie. This means a lot." The music began; I looked over to see Tim behind all of the equipment, smiling happily. "Is that your boyfriend?" Bob asked.

"I think so." *I hope so.*

"He looks, um, okay."

Garrauch, who it turns out is even bossier than any of the rest of us, arranged us in order and admonished us to stand up straight. "You must walk like swans, ladies. You will not waddle like geese!" I lifted my beak and stretched my swan neck gracefully as Tyler took my arm.

"This is much better, Mom. Having Dad here to walk with Jenna. Me walking with you."

"Were you afraid I wouldn't make it down the aisle by myself?"

"No, not that, though I did promise Auntie Gwen that I wouldn't let you trip." Tyler smiled. "It's just that we're all together again. Our family."

He was right. This was better. Maybe we wouldn't be celebrating Fourth of July together. Maybe we would never be as free and easy as we had once been. Maybe I wouldn't be invited to be in the wedding party if Bob and Clarisse got married (thank God!). But at least the tension had been broken. The kids could once again have both parents together when they needed them.

Our cue came and we headed down the aisle (I wonder why it's never "up the aisle"?) and took our places. The minister stood on a riser with Ryan nervously waiting just below him. The music changed, and Jenna made her entrance.

So let me just take a few moments (or a month or two if you have the time) to tell you just how beautiful my daughter looked coming down the aisle on her wedding day. Remember Grace Kelly in *High Society?* Audrey Hepburn in *Roman Holiday?* Young Jackie Kennedy? Princess Di? None of them come even close to how extraordinary Jenna looked that day.

Her beautiful blue hair was iridescent, adorned with flowers gathered from the nearby meadow. Lilah's, now Jenna's, enchanting wedding dress in shimmering silk charmeuse was reminiscent of Carole Lombard with a deep cowl draping gracefully in both the front and back. It made Jenna look sophisticated and innocent, sexy and sweet. My daughter's big brown eyes were luminous in the soft light of the open tent; her face glowed as she walked confidently next to her father toward us. She kissed her dad, took Ryan's hand with a radiant smile, and passed me her bouquet.

"I love you, Mom," she whispered. "I brought this for you." She handed me a large hanky, dish-towel size. How did she know?

"I love you too, sweetheart," I whispered back, putting the hanky to immediate use.

"Dearly Beloved, we are gathered here . . ."

"Wait!" Jenna cried, cutting off the minister. What now? She whispered something in Ryan's ear; Ryan smiled and conferred with the minister. The three of them shuffled around, exchanging places so that Jenna and Ryan faced out to the audience.

"Hi, Gran!" Jenna grinned and waved. She nodded to the minister. "Okay, I'm ready now. You were saying?"

Epilogue

There is something incredibly delicious in that moment when you first take off your shoes after a big event. Especially if the big event went exceptionally well and you are in the company of your very best friends.

"So, Angie, you did it. Your beautiful little girl had the perfect wedding." Gwen looked a touch fuzzy, having downed a few glasses of the exquisite champagne she had scored for the event.

" 'I' didn't do it, my friends. 'We' did."

"She's right," Jess mumbled. "You're nothing without us, Angie."

"Hmmm." I felt a little warm in the spring heat and fanned myself with a napkin.

"Look at Lilah, making the moves on that interesting gentleman with the ponytail. We could take lessons from her," Marie noted.

Lilah and Tom were cutting the rug in grand style. I was sure that his fire hose was fully functional, and I figured that Lilah might have an interesting night ahead of her. It was getting warmer; I placed an ice cube from my glass on my forehead.

"Who is that beautiful young woman with Tyler?" Gwen asked.

"Angeline. Tom's granddaughter. American Indian. McGeorge second year. Watch out for her, Gwen. She's very bright."

"Hmmm. A keeper then? I was thinking that I should get an intern for the summer. Think she'd be interested?"

"Perhaps." I smiled knowing that Auntie Gwen would make sure that Tyler's love interest had local, gainful employment.

"Aren't they cute? Will you look at our boys?" Marie pointed across the room at a group standing at the bar. Jack, Tim, Wayne, and . . . Whatsis Name?

"Jess, now that Whatsis name is back in your life, don't you think we should know what his name is?" I asked.

"Wait." Jess lifted up her sleeve and looked at an inked scribble on her wrist. "Keith. His name is Keith."

We took a moment, thinking about the men in our lives. Thinking about our futures with and without them. My forehead felt damp, and I felt a rush of heat rising from my chest. Maybe I'd had too much to drink . . .

"Oh, look! She's getting ready to throw the bouquet!" Gwen pulled me to my feet.

"Who knows, Angie?" Marie's eyes twinkled as she pushed me from behind. "You might be next."

The heat was becoming extreme. I felt my face flush and the sweat pour down my front.

"Is it just me, or is it becoming uncomfortably hot in here?"

Want More?

Turn the page to enter
Avon's Little Black Book —

the dish, the scoop and the
cherry on top from
HEATHER ESTAY

Q & A with Heather Estay

Heather Estay, author of *It's Never Too Late to Be a Bridesmaid,* grew up in Denver, Colorado. She moved to northern California in 1969 to attend Stanford University and has been there ever since (based on her unwillingness to shovel snow and her aversion to fuzzy hats with earflaps).

She graduated from Stanford with a degree in psychology, but, realizing that her personal philosophy of "just get over it and get on with it!" would not endear her to many clients, she pursued alternate avenues of employment. Among other things, Heather bought houses and remodeled them, taught martial arts, and had a short stint operating a shrink-wrap machine (she claims that she has since recovered from the fumes). Her seventeen years in commercial real estate finally drove her to the brink, motivating her to find a career where she could spend all day muttering to herself in her pajamas: a career as a writer.

Heather is unintentionally single and resides in Sacramento, California. *Little Black Book* talked with her there for this interview:

Where do you get the ideas for your books? From life, mine and other people's. I am such a voyeur! Honestly, you don't need to create "a Martian zombie heiress who runs for city council and schemes to eliminate the competition by luring local alligators out of the swamp to eat them" to create a plot that is slightly off the wall. There are plenty of bizarre story lines in ordinary lives, from those of us who are presumed to be normal. The zombie alligator thing probably wouldn't happen in your neighborhood, right? (Okay, maybe it's more likely for those of you in Florida.) But you might be able to see yourself or one of your friends flipping out and ending up in jail, or ranting and raving on the courthouse steps. (Unless you and your friends are more sane than my friends and I are . . .)

I also don't write about *Dynasty* people. The ones who are so smart, so beautiful, so wealthy, so accomplished, so sophisticated. That's just not my life. I honestly can't tell the difference between a Prada and a Gucci, and I don't think I'm the only one in the universe who can't. (I am? No kidding.) It's fun to read about The Rich and Famous, but sometimes those characters seem as connected to my reality as that alien zombie heiress.

So what is this second book about? What's its main theme?

Ah! My editor, after she read the first draft, asked me the same thing. I don't know that it's really "about" anything. But I'll tell you some of the ideas that prompted it.

First of all, when I wrote *It's Never Too Late to Get a Life,* I was strongly advised to make the Angie character younger (originally, she was fifty-two, my age at the time). I pushed back and we compromised by making her forty-nine. But I chafed doing it. I guess the prevailing wisdom is that not many people would be interested in the romantic misadventures or lives of anyone over fifty.

Well, I'm clearly no marketing guru, but I know scads of women around my age who are interesting, sexy, active, and funny. And we read! Most of us are not trying to reclaim lost youth; we've been there and done that. So at this stage in our lives, we enjoy reading about us, who we are now.

I've been in my thirties, and I've done the forties. Now I'm fiftysomething, and I LIKE it here. Some of my issues remain the same: my hair will not stay fluffed for more than twenty-six minutes, my nose gets unbelievably red and ugly when I cry, and I still find myself doing every no-no outlined in *He's Just Not That Into You.*

But some things are pleasantly different at this age. For instance, the men in my age range, though they tend toward more hair in their ears than on their heads (for those of you who are unaware of this phenomenon, it hits around their late forties), the odds are also greater that they've had vasectomies—yahoo! And you don't have to worry if he's going to get old and fat because, well, he already is or he isn't (and so are you). And some of the clues to his character are clearer: if he's often unemployed, living with his mother, never been married, and unfamiliar with the dishwasher at age fifty, well, you can be pretty sure that what you see is what you'll get. (This is probably true if he is thirtysomething, too, but it's easier to kid yourself about a man still in his thirties.)

And at this age, we're not worried so much about ourselves getting married; we're planning weddings for our kids. We tend to have a lighter grasp on whatever career ladder we're climbing. Typically, the only little ones we have underfoot are grandkids who can be returned to their owners at the end of the day. And, most important, we've figured out which friends are really keepers because we've seen each other through many seasons.

So I think it's just fine and dandy to be over forty and wanted to say so. I used menopause because it seems to be the final demarcation between "vital and sexy" and "you still around, Grandma?" (Europeans seem to feel differently about this. I don't know why. Maybe it's genetic. Those elderly European queens were famous for lopping off heads of men who didn't adore them. The only men who survived to procreate were the ones smart enough to adore elderly queens.) And menopause symptoms are extreme and funny (though perhaps more funny in retrospect), kind of like that Vulcan disease where a Vulcan male gets whacked out and goes nuts every seven years. It is the ultimate PMS for many of us, a Ripley's Believe It or Not stage of life that we ALL end up going through. (The Universe has a great sense of humor.)

Another issue that occurred to me as I was writing the book is that our lives, at any age, are not always our own, know what I mean? Sometimes the dramas (or comedies) of our friends and families take over, or the urgencies of our jobs take precedence over our personal agenda. At those times, the tidy personal To-Do list we start on Monday morning falls apart by midafternoon and never recovers.

Personally, I'm sure this is why I haven't learned Spanish/meditated more/trained my beagles/etc., and why my dating life is so dismal. (If, by some miracle, I am dating a wonderful man when this book comes out: Honey, I'm not talking about you.) Those activities take focus, time, and energy, none of which I ever seem to have in excess. First, the kid needs help in school. Then the six-month project for work has to get finished within two. My beagle needs knee surgery; my buddy is falling apart from a rough divorce; my roof is leaking, and mice are invading the pantry. So? All my personal extracurricular activities take a back burner, along with my housecleaning and that regular flossing I've always meant to do.

So what is your creative process? Do you have a system for writing?

Gosh, now that I've written two whole books, I'm obviously an expert on this. Right now, I begin each book with an idea that makes me laugh. Then I get all excited about it and put together an outline that my agent and editor get all excited about. Then I sit down to write it and spend the next several weeks wondering: What the heck was I thinking? I'm not a writer! I have no idea how this could all come together! Do you suppose they have openings at Walmart?

Next, after several weeks of wholehearted self-flagellation and four dozen (or so) boxes of Twinkies, I sit down, put together a rough outline, rough out some scenes, etc. From then on, I intersperse days of Twinkie-bingeing/self-flagellation with days of actually doing something productive until the book is done.

Honestly, I'm not a writer. If anything, someday I'd love to be considered a humorist, a storyteller. My idols for this are people like Mark Twain and Erma Bombeck. I also adore Will Rogers (though that rope twirling thing is beyond me) and I think that Dave Barry should remain on this planet as long as his extraterrestrial handlers will allow.

My first goal is to make things I write relatable. I'm hoping you could say, "Oh, yeah, I know someone like that" or "I can just see myself doing that!" My second goal is to make you laugh out loud at least once or twice. (Humor is a tricky thing, definitely a matter of taste. But so is anything: literature, fashion, Braunschweiger. You can't really claim something is funny or it's not funny. Pee Wee Herman never did much for me; Noel Coward did. Half of America would disagree with me on that one.) My third goal is to make you feel just a little bit better about life in general when you've finished the book.

In the little bit of writing I've done so far, here's what I'm learning: Write so that I enjoy it. Don't worry too much about what other people may like or dislike. (I doubt any good work comes from being too conscious of the polls.) Write so that if my mother reads it, she won't disown me. And write things that might embarrass my son (that's not really a writing tip, I just think it's my maternal duty).

So what's next for you?

Well, I'm just finishing the third (and the last) in this series. It's to be called *It's Never Too Late to Something or Other*.

I've got a few zillion ideas for other books in my head. The trick is to get them out of my head and on paper. I'll probably need to buy stock in whoever makes Twinkies (is it General Motors?) to do so.

And I've got to go out and buy some new jammies; these are just about worn through.

And now here's a sneak peek at Angie's third adventure, available soon from Avon Trade!

"Oh, look! She's getting ready to throw the bouquet!" Gwen pulled me to my feet.

"Who knows, Angie?" Marie's eyes twinkled as she pushed me from behind. "You might be next."

The heat was becoming extreme. I felt my face flush and the sweat pour down my front.

"Is it just me or is it becoming uncomfortably hot in here?"

"Later, Angie!" Jessica's face lit up with excitement as she yanked me into the crush of panting single females. "Get ready for the catch!"

Jenna, my beautiful daughter, waved her bridal bouquet like a matador's red cape, taunting the herd of half-crazed bulls (uh, make that cows). She turned her back to us as the crowd shouted the countdown:

"One! Two! Three!"

Jenna lofted the bouquet high over her shoulder. Up, up, up it went and landed with a soft *plop* in Jessica's hands.

"Eeek!" Jess squeaked in panic, swatting at the flowers as if they were Venus flytraps out for her blood. The bouquet flew with adamant trajectory into Gwen's open arms.

"Ugh!" Frantically, Gwen launched the hapless spray of roses into the air. It flew gracefully over the ceiling fan, pausing dramatically before it reentered the stratosphere and headed straight for me.

"Yaaa!" I pitched it back to Gwen instantly, a well-trained first baseman in the last game of the World Series.

For the next thirty seconds, the three of us batted that bouquet back and forth desperately, a good imitation of the US Olympic Volleyball team in a life-and-death game of Hot Potato. Suddenly, a huge purple rhino charged into the fracas with a ferocious body block. The force was great enough to send all three of us spiraling into Marie, who (though innocent of any bouquet batting) is one of our very best friends and therefore certainly would be thrilled to join us in the resulting pileup.

"I got it! I got it!" the rhino, Clarisse, yelled triumphantly. She held her trophy, the sadly battered bridal bouquet, high above her head.

Jessica, Gwen, Marie, and I lay panting, arms and legs entwined, a tangled purple heap of middle-aged bridesmaids.

"What on earth was that all about?" Marie demanded, her head mashed under Jessica's left hip. She did not sound at all thrilled to have joined us there.

"Angie! For God's sake, say something so I know you're alive!" Tim exclaimed anxiously. He, along with Jack, Whatsis Name, and Wayne, nervously sorted through the jumble of their significant others' legs and arms, searching for a familiar limb to pull out of the purple wreckage.

"Angie! I'm coming!" Bob bellowed, muscling his way into the fray. ("Muscling" is probably inaccurate given my ex's anatomy, but I've never heard of anyone "flabbing" their way through a crowd.) He stumbled over Tim, ensnared himself in the folds of Clarisse's purple caftan, then skidded halfway across the dance floor before crashing into our new son-in-law and the remains of the six-tiered wedding cake.

"Mom," Tyler laughed, pulling me to my shaky feet, "aren't you and the aunties getting a little old for tackle football? How about taking up Tai Chi instead?"

In retrospect (isn't it a waste to have such brilliant hindsight and such pathetic foresight?), I know that those bizarre moments were a forewarning of the year to come. Had I known that then, I would have left the party immediately and crawled into a cave to hibernate until the following spring (or until my gray hairs overpowered my most recent application of Miss Clairol, whichever came first).

But I didn't. Instead, I joined Gwen, Marie, and Jess in polishing off another bottle of champagne. Big mistake. *Really* big mistake.

HEATHER ESTAY

HEATHER ESTAY lives in Sacremento, California, with her roommates, Spud and Alli (two beagles who bear absolutely no resemblance to the beagles in her books—ha!). *It's Never Too Late to Be a Bridesmaid* is her second attempt at humorous fiction, which she writes to support her golf addiction. If you buy this book, she may also be able to pay her rent.